BAY STREET BLOOD

By Edward Hill

 FriesenPress

Suite 300 - 990 Fort St
Victoria, BC, V8V 3K2
Canada

www.friesenpress.com

Copyright © 2020 by Edward Hill
First Edition — 2020

All rights reserved.

No part of this publication may be reproduced in any form, or by any means, electronic or mechanical, including photocopying, recording, or any information browsing, storage, or retrieval system, without permission in writing from FriesenPress.

ISBN
978-1-5255-6418-5 (Hardcover)
978-1-5255-6419-2 (Paperback)
978-1-5255-6420-8 (eBook)

Fiction, Thriller

Distributed to the trade by The Ingram Book Company

FOR MARCIA

*To know her
was to love her*

*Enthusiastic thanks to
Linda Pygiel
who single-handedly bridged the gulf
between a quill-pen author
and a 21st century publisher*

placed a reassuring hand on the man's shoulder. "We're just here for a quick one, George. Do you have an out-of-the-way corner?"

George's smile reappeared. "Right this way, Dr. Manetti." George was more than happy to park O'Malley in an "out-of-the-way corner."

O'Malley told the waiter he'd have whatever Manetti was having. Then he lounged back with a self-conscious smirk and began to mimic George. "*Right this way, Dr. Manetti.* What's all this doctor bullshit? You're in the minin' business."

"I'm a rock doctor, Paddy."

"Well there's nothin' wrong with my rocks, doc." O'Malley guffawed loudly and then began to study the vista. "You sure hang out in ritzy places, *Doctor* Manetti." The waiter arrived with two glasses of Mill Street lager. "Fancy view! Fancy beer! Fancy car! Fancy beard! *Fancy* all the way 'round, I'd say."

"Cheers, Paddy! Now what's on your mind?"

"It's a long story."

"Make it a short story."

O'Malley drained half his glass in one go and then wiped his mouth with the back of his hand. "I owe some money to a nasty, and he wants to get paid."

"A loan shark?"

"I guess you could call him that ... somethin' like that."

"And you want me to bail you out."

O'Malley nodded. "It's not much, Rocco ... just five grand. Just a loan, eh?"

It was Manetti's turn to mimic. *"Just a loan, eh?* And just whom will you hit up to repay me?"

O'Malley gazed out across Lake Ontario and ignored the question.

"Apart from the five thousand, are your finances all right?"

"Sure! Sure!"

"Somehow your *Sure! Sure!* doesn't fill me with confidence, Paddy." Manetti studied O'Malley's face for a moment. Then he took a cheque from his billfold and quickly filled it in. "I'll bail you out, Paddy, for *Auld Lang Syne*, but only this once. *Capisce?*"

As O'Malley reached for the cheque, Manetti pulled it back. "I want to hear it from you, Paddy. *Only this once.*"

"Sure! Sure!"

"*Sure! Sure!* doesn't do it, Paddy. *Only this once!* Let's hear it."

"Sure! Sure! Only this once."

"You taught me a lot about hockey ... way back when." He handed the cheque to O'Malley. "That's a one-time, one-off coaching fee. *Capisce?*"

"Sure! Sure! Thanks Rocco. You're a life saver, eh?"

Manetti picked up his glass and sat back. "I guess I haven't seen you since you hung up your skates; let's see, that'd be around 1995, right?"

"Ninety-seven!" retorted O'Malley, his aggrieved tone suggesting that the event was emblazoned on the national memory. "Actually, the last time I seen you was seventy-four."

"That long ago, was it? I was at Queen's in 1974, working at Big Nickel in the summers. Well, Paddy, I've seen *you* many times since 1974. We hockey fans see our hockey heroes, but alas, our hockey heroes see only the faceless crowd. I used to see you at the Gardens when Detroit was in town. It always took me back to our hockey days in Sudbury. Always made me wonder whether I could have made the NHL too."

"You could have, but you blew your chances by goin' to college."

"I was probably too small for the NHL."

"So was Gretsky."

"Thanks for the comparison. I guess I just paid for it."

"You weren't no Gretsky, but you could have made the NHL. You could handle the puck, and you were a fast skater. How come you never stopped by at the Gardens? Too stuck up to come 'round and say hello, that's why."

"Actually, I did once, but I didn't stay. I felt conspicuous standing there with all those kids looking for autographs ... and their older sisters looking for romance."

"Lookin' to get laid, you mean." O'Malley looked wistful. "Yeah, there were always lots of girls."

"Anyway, Paddy, we're both old farts now. What have you been doing with yourself since ninety-seven?"

"Not much; bummin' around mostly." O'Malley drained his glass. "Livin' on my NHL pension, though it's not much to live on." He stared soulfully at the empty glass, but his host ignored both him and the hovering waiter.

"Look, I'd like to have another drink and reminisce about the good old days, but I've got to get on my way." Manetti stood up. "Maybe we can do it another time."

"Sure! Sure! We'll get together ... some time real soon." O'Malley picked up his host's half-empty glass and drained it. "Waste not, want not, I always say." Then he got to his feet with a slight stagger and followed Manetti out of the bar.

When they reached the main floor rotunda, Manetti ended the interview. "Good luck, Paddy. Stay clear of loan sharks." They shook hands.

"So long for now, Rocco, but we've still got lots to talk about. Like you said, we should get together and 'reminisce about the good old days'."

As he watched O'Malley shamble off towards King Street, Manetti realized that he'd just been threatened.

5

CHAPTER
TWO

ALTHOUGH WILLIAM GRAYDON routinely kept people waiting, he himself was seldom kept waiting. After all, he was Managing Director of Thorne Sullivan Canada. However, he and Jill Armstrong were being kept waiting today – intentionally kept waiting - or so Graydon thought.

They were at the appointed place: the Toronto offices of Lunex Inc. They had presented themselves at the appointed date and time, August 27, ten a.m., but nothing was happening.

Upon arrival, they'd been ushered into a conference room by a pleasant young woman who had introduced herself as Ann Stevenson and informed them apologetically that Dr. Manetti was detained on a conference call and would join them shortly. She had then poured coffee and left them on their own—Armstrong waiting patiently; Graydon waiting impatiently.

Graydon usually circulated with an entourage of two or three lieutenants, but today he'd selected just one—albeit a glamorous one. Today was not the day to overwhelm Manetti with a team of investment bankers. Today was the day for a low-key interview, an affable interview, if it ever got started. As things were turning out, he was secretly relieved that only one of his juniors was there to witness this indignity to Graydon the Great.

At 10:20, Ann Stevenson reappeared to renew the apology. She poured more coffee and left them with a plate of cookies.

By 10:30, Graydon had read *The Wall Street Journal*, cover to cover, and was decidedly restive.

By 10:40, he was very restless indeed, and thoroughly convinced that the delay was an intentional discourtesy.

By 10:45, he was pacing the floor and fighting back a strong desire to walk out. He desperately wanted to trump Manetti's let-them-wait card by walking out, but he dared not sacrifice his client's interests on the altar of personal pique, lest his client sacrifice Thorne Sullivan on the same altar. He'd have to grin and bear it.

In sharp contrast to her boss, Jill Armstrong was busy with another file, quite unperturbed by the delay. If and when the interview got started, her job was to have all relevant details at her fingertips and to feed that information smoothly into the discussion in response to Graydon's cues. Graydon had all the relevant details at his own fingertips, but it was beneath his dignity to deal in petty details—except in his own office and at the expense of his underlings.

Unlike the luxurious reception rooms at Thorne Sullivan Canada, this Lunex conference room was decidedly workaday. The main piece of furniture was a large and somewhat battered teak table, surrounded by six leather swivel chairs. The table was cluttered with a telephone, a slide projector, a pile of note pads, a mug of pens and pencils, two files belonging to Jill Armstrong, one *Wall Street Journal* belonging to Bill Graydon, two coffee cups, and a plate of cookies.

One wall of the room was completely taken up by a set of teak cabinets; a second was cork panelled for geological-map-mounting; a third was reserved for a retractable screen; and the fourth was the window wall. The only decorations in the room, if they could be called decorations, were a dozen or so unframed photographs pinned at random along either side of the cork wall—enlarged snapshots showing groups of hirsute men in bush gear, standing in front of float planes or tents or rock outcroppings.

It was a down-to-work workplace, except for the window wall, with its view of Lake Ontario—a lake drenched in sunshine today and dotted with sails. It was summertime out there, and the sailing fraternity was celebrating.

Graydon looked around dismissively, and then yawned dismissively. The boss was bored as well as irritated. "If this room is as good as it gets, I think Lunex should go exploring for a decorator. You're on our decorating committee, Armstrong. How would you describe this place?"

Thus summoned, Armstrong closed her file and studied the room for a moment. "Rich jocks, no taste, macho macho, fully depreciated ... but it has a nice view."

"Yes, the south side of the TD Tower is scenic and restful."

"I wouldn't know."

"We put you on the north side, so you'll keep your mind on mergers and acquisitions instead of sailboats and sailors. I have my office on the south side, so I can restfully supervise you north-siders."

Armstrong made a face and crossed the room to take a closer look at the photographs. "There's one man who's front and centre in all these pictures," she said. "Fairly slim with a narrow beard. I assume that's Dr. Manetti."

"That's our man."

"Does he always wear a beard?"

"Yes, and he always dresses like that, like he's in a bush camp somewhere ... or like a wannabe Fidel Castro."

"He's much better looking than Castro, and much better groomed ... and he seems happy in these pictures. Castro never looks happy."

"Manetti always looks to me like a model for Tilley Endurables."

"Is he as good as they say?" she asked. "Unless our background file's exaggerating, he's fast becoming a living legend in the mining industry."

Graydon looked displeased. "Perhaps our research people got a little carried away. He's a brilliant explorationist, I have to grant him that, and he's made a roaring success of Lunex."

"I see the original name was *Lungarno Exploration*. I wonder why they changed it?"

"They accepted the inevitable. They adopted the brokers' acronym, in their case, *Lunex.*"

"Too bad! *Lungarno's* a much better name than Lunex. I wonder if Dr. Manetti has family ties to Florence?"

"Italy somewhere." Graydon shrugged. "In my view, Lungarno is a stupid name for a gold-exploration company in North America, which is probably another reason why they changed it."

"Why *stupid?*"

"Because it has nothing to do with gold or exploration or mining or North America. *Lungarno Dredging* would be a good name for a dredging company in Florence. *Lungarno Towers* would be a good name for an apartment building in Florence. *Lungarno's* a stupid name for any company in Canada, except perhaps an Italian restaurant."

"I like *Lungaro Exploration.* It has old-world charm and intrigue. There must be a romantic story behind that name."

"*Charm! Intrigue! Romance!* You should have gone into advertising instead of investment banking. I bet you'd buy an overpriced frock from an outfit calling itself *Lungarno Fashions.* Anyway, why don't you ask Manetti? Maybe he'll tell you the *romantic story* ... if he deigns to show up."

She continued to study the photographs. "There's a younger man who shows up in most of these pictures but never front and centre."

"That's Warren Ransom. You should have done your homework; they're both in the file."

"Not their photographs."

"Their photographs are in the Lunex annual report, which is in the file."

Her back was turned, so Graydon didn't see her tongue sticking out. "I did my homework," she said. "He's number two at Lunex and, like Manetti, is reputed to be a genius geologist."

"These cowboys may be geniuses ... or they may be just lucky. Either way, they've discovered Eldorado North ... and we want it."

"Did you tell Manetti why we're here?"

"No, but I'm sure he knows. That's why he's left us cooling our heels."

"When he does show up, I take it you're not expecting a friendly reception."

"*If* he shows up, I expect you and I will be shown the door in short order. However, our job is to fire a shot across Manetti's bow ... to let him know, as diplomatically as possible, that Noramet means business."

"Is there anything I should know before you start firing? Anything not in the backgrounder?"

"One thing, perhaps, although I don't know much about it myself. Since you've done your homework, you'll have noted that Manetti worked for Noramet back in the eighties. He was only there a few years and then quit abruptly ... somewhere around 1985."

"1984."

Graydon glared at her.

"The file doesn't say anything about *abruptly*," she added quickly.

"No, it doesn't, but he did. Dick Fennell didn't tell me the whys and wherefores, but there's some bad blood there somewhere."

"Shouldn't we know those whys and wherefores? I mean, that's important background information."

"Yes, we should, and yes, it is. However, what Dick Fennell wants you to know, he tells you. What he doesn't want you to know, he doesn't tell you. Apparently, he doesn't want to tell us why Manetti quit Noramet."

"Maybe we'll find out today."

"Maybe."

"I see in the backgrounder that Warren Ransom is also an alumnus of Noramet," she said.

"Yes, but there's no bad blood between him and Dick. At least, as far as I know, there isn't."

She continued to examine the photographs. "Dr. Manetti has a nice smile in those pictures, but he looks tough all the same."

"Sure, he's tough," said Graydon, "but is he *smart tough* or *stubborn tough*? *Smart tough* people we can handle. *Stubborn tough* people often damn the torpedoes, which means we have to fire the torpedoes and sink their ships. That's messy for everyone. My gut tells me Manetti will prove to be *stubborn tough*, which is too bad for him … and for us too. My gut tells me this takeover is going to be messy. We'll soon—"

Just then, their host burst into the room. "Please forgive me!" The two men shook hands. "It took well over an hour to choke off a conference call that should only have lasted ten minutes. I do apologize."

"No problem!" said Graydon, forcing a smile. "We've been working away on our files." He handed Manetti two business cards. "May I introduce my colleague, Jill Armstrong."

Manetti and Armstrong shook hands as Graydon continued. "As you probably know, we're neighbours in the Toronto Dominion Tower. We have the forty-fourth and forty-fifth floors of the building."

"Yes, I see Thorne Sullivan's name on the building register. It's amazing that people on different floors of the same building never seem to cross paths."

"It's the pace of business in downtown Toronto—the ever-accelerating pace. We're getting as bad as New York, with everybody rushing, nobody strolling. However, you and I did cross paths recently, albeit briefly, at the Mining Hall of Fame dinner."

"Yes, of course," replied Manetti, who obviously didn't remember.

"Let me congratulate you again on your induction."

"Thank you. However, I think they were only recognizing the grey in my beard."

"To the contrary," said Graydon, "it was a well-deserved recognition by your peers."

Manetti shrugged. "If you hang around long enough, they elect you out of sympathy. As far as I'm concerned, the worst part of those events is having to wear a dinner jacket and having to listen to all those phoney tributes. Anyway, Lunex is honoured to be visited by our illustrious neighbour, and I apologize again for keeping you waiting." He paused to glance at the cards. "Since you're managing director, and since Ms. Armstrong seems to concern herself with mergers and acquisitions, I assume you're here to talk about mergers and acquisitions, so ... let's make up for lost time."

Armstrong suppressed a smile, recognising that Graydon was just getting into gear. To ask Graydon to leave off the small talk and name dropping was to ask a Vladimir Horowitz to come away from his piano.

"Well then," said Graydon, looking flustered, "to get right down to cases, we're representing Noramet Inc., which is interested in your Mountain Lake properties and—"

"Of course they are," interrupted Manetti. "The whole world's watching Mountain Lake."

"Yes, but unlike the rest of the world, Noramet has adjacent properties, as well as a nearby mine, and a smelter operating just six miles away. The synergies are quite incredible ... but of course, you know all that."

"I know where the Otter Lake mine and smelter are located. I know that Noramet has properties to the north of us, and I know where they've been drilling. That's all I know."

"We've been asked to ascertain whether you're interested, *in principle,* in either selling your Mountain Lake properties outright or entering into a joint venture arrangement with Noramet."

"Speaking for myself, the answer is *no* and *no* … not *in principle* or any other way. We have yet to define the exact size and shape of the orebody, and we don't yet know whether the initial indications of grade will hold up. These are early days. We have a good two years of hard work ahead of us." Manetti beamed a disingenuous smile. "Lunex certainly wouldn't want to sell Noramet a pig-in-a-poke."

"Noramet knows a little bit about the gold business," replied Graydon, "and it knows that Mountain Lake is no *pig-in-a-poke*. Noramet believes it can assist and accelerate the exploration and development work."

"Thanks anyway. We have all the expertise we need, and we can raise all the capital we need. A joint venture would make sense, if we shared the same orebody, but we don't. Tell Richard Fennell that our orebody is trending away from the Noramet properties, and tell him that, even if it weren't, his approach is premature. You can't snatch the baby before the baby's born."

"Noramet isn't trying to snatch the baby," said Graydon. "Noramet wants to ensure the child's future."

"With respect, I think the only future of concern to Richard Fennell is Richard Fennell's." Manetti turned to Jill Armstrong. "Would you put your baby up for adoption before it was born?"

"Perhaps the metaphor distorts the realities," she replied frostily. "I mean, Lunex is an exploration company, and in the normal course, Lunex can be expected to sell the Mountain Lake orebody to a gold producer. Noramet's Otter Lake operations offer synergies to Noramet, which no other producer enjoys … as Bill indicated." She glanced at Graydon, who took the handoff.

"Jill's quite right. No matter how you slice it, Mountain Lake is worth more to Noramet than it is to any other producer, and Noramet can and will be the highest bidder. So, given those dynamics, it may not be premature to explore mutually satisfactory contractual arrangements."

"You're assuming Mountain Lake is for sale." Manetti stared at them thoughtfully. "In my view, you *are* trying to snatch the baby. The metaphor may seem inept to you, but to me it seems quite apt. However, since Ms. Armstrong apparently dislikes the metaphor—or at least thinks it *distorts the realities*—let's abandon the metaphor and look at the realities from a Lunex perspective. Let's look at my company, a team of highly-skilled, highly-motivated, hard-working explorationists who've discovered a significant orebody and are working flat out to define it. Now, *right in the midst of that work*, Richard Fennell picks up the telephone in New York and despatches his Toronto investment bankers to scoop the prize, or at least to try. Those are the realities as I see them."

"With respect, Noramet isn't trying to *snatch a baby*, nor is it trying to *scoop a prize*," replied Graydon, his voice betraying irritation.

Armstrong interrupted, a deft attempt to ease the tension. "I have a question, Dr. Manetti."

"Shoot!"

"It has nothing to do with Mountain Lake, I'm afraid."

"All the better."

"Before you came in, Bill and I were speculating about the original name of your company, *Lungarno Exploration*. I said there must be a romantic story attached to the name."

"And what did Mr. Graydon say?"

"He said you might tell me."

Manetti tilted his chair and studied the ceiling for a long moment; then he tilted back. "The story's not a romance, Ms. Armstrong, it's a tragedy. During the Second World War, my grandfather and father were part of the underground movement to liberate Florence. My father found my grandfather's corpse sprawled on Lungarno Torrigiani, not far from their home. He'd been gunned down by a German street patrol."

Graydon turned red and Armstrong turned white.

"I'm so sorry," she said. "I shouldn't have asked."

15

"No reason you shouldn't have asked. Actually, you're the first outsider with curiosity enough to ask. My father was understandably traumatized by that tragedy, and *Lungarno* was my way of paying tribute to my father, whom I loved, and to my grandfather, whom I never knew."

"That's a wonderful tribute," replied Armstrong. "Why did you change the name?"

"Stock brokers can't handle long names, so they called us Lunex … and Lunex we became. My parents were both dead by that time, so the tribute had served its purpose. Now it's a coded tribute to a man who was murdered by the Nazis."

"Acronyms have overtaken a lot of proud names," said Graydon, "*Inco, Alcan, Dofasco, Stelco…*"

"And foreigners have taken over those proud names," interjected Manetti.

Graydon ignored the comment. "I've always thought that the *Noramet* acronym was a trivial substitute for *North American Metals*."

"Speaking of foreigners," said Manetti, "we should get back to business. What's next?"

"Well, Dick Fennell asked us to develop and analyze structures that might be of mutual interest and benefit to Lunex and Noramet, and then to bring them forward for your consideration."

"*Develop and analyze structures,*" echoed Manetti. "Forgive me but that sounds like investment bankers' bafflegab. I don't want to be gratuitously insulting—I really don't—but the problem I have with investment bankers is that they never run the businesses they buy and sell. They never get their hands dirty. You 'develop and analyze structures,' whatever that means. You talk about the 'efficient use of capital, and maximizing shareholder value,' which more often than not, are euphemisms for exploitation and anti-competitive aggression. In this case, Mountain Lake is your intended prey, which is why I'm being so blunt."

"With respect, if investment bankers didn't serve a useful function, we wouldn't exist," retorted Graydon.

"Same goes for hit men," said Manetti.

Graydon reddened, but his voice didn't betray his irritation. "You don't have to be a hockey player to sell a hockey franchise. In fact, hockey players wouldn't know the first thing about selling a hockey franchise."

"True, but they know how to play hockey, and they'd know whether the franchise needed selling. In my experience, many investment bankers devote their formidable talents to breaking up or re-organizing companies that are doing just fine and should be left alone. They do their dirty work for fat fees, and on behalf of predators, who are trying to corner larger market share by eliminating smaller competitors."

"I'm sorry you have such a low opinion of our profession," said Graydon, "and I'm somewhat surprised, since I believe Lunex retains Bailey North, an excellent firm of investment bankers."

"We do, and they are. We use them as a shield to protect us from other investment bankers. In this case, they predicted you'd be showing up, and here you are."

"Here we are indeed." Graydon was no longer trying to mask his irritation. "Well then, I'll advise Noramet that you're not interested in its proposal."

"Speaking for myself, that's correct. However, I'm only the CEO, so if Richard Fennell has a formal proposal to make, let him make it. I'll certainly take it to my Board."

"But you wouldn't recommend it to your Board."

"I haven't seen the proposal. However, I've been frank with you about my views—perhaps too frank. I apologize for insulting your profession; I realize you have a job to do."

"Well then," said Graydon, "I'll report back to Noramet that you're not interested *in principle* but will take any formal proposal to the Lunex Board. Is that accurate?"

"Tell Richard Fennell that I'm highly disinterested *in principle*, and find it hard to imagine a formal proposal I would recommend to my Board, although I'll certainly hold my nose and take any formal proposal to the Lunex Directors. I have no choice."

"Message received," said Graydon. "Noramet's preferred option is to buy your Mountain Lake properties outright, or failing that, to enter into a joint venture with Lunex. However, I'd be remiss if I didn't tell you that our client reserves the right to consider other options."

"Message received," replied Manetti.

"I notice that you always refer to Dick Fennell rather than Noramet," said Graydon. "Do you know Dick then?"

"Yes, and I know how he operates. I'm an alumnus of Noramet, as I'm sure you both know. At the risk of offending Ms. Armstrong, tell Richard Fennell that the gestation period for this baby will be at least two years, and if it's a good-looking kid, maybe we'll raise the little bastard ourselves. Who knows? Maybe it's time for us to re-invent Lunex. Maybe it's time for Lunex to become a gold producer in its own right ... or maybe we should become investment bankers."

Manetti stood up, followed by Graydon and Armstrong. The interview was over. The three shook hands again, and Manetti walked them to the elevator lobby. Once there, he put a hand on Graydon's shoulder, as if to impart a confidence. "About Noramet's *other options,* tell your friend Dick to consult the Old Testament, the first book of Samuel. He'll find my answer in Chapter 17, verses 37 and 49. Nice to meet you Ms. Armstrong."

And so it came to pass that the Noramet emissaries went forth from that place even unto their own place, wondering aloud what message there was in the first book of Samuel.

And lo, their librarian came unto them with an Old Testament, whereupon the emissaries seized it and read the cited verses but liked them not.

And they reported to Richard Fennell the third, he being known as Dick, what Manetti had told them, and they were sore afraid when they read aloud to Dick the verses which Manetti had cited:

> *"David said moreover, The Lord that delivered me out of the paw of the lion, and out of the paw of the bear, he will deliver me out of the hand of the Philistine..."*

> *"And David put his hand in his bag, and took thence a stone, and slang it, and smote the Philistine in his forehead, that the stone sank into his forehead; and he fell upon his face to the earth."*

And Dick was angered by the verses and vowed vengeance.

CHAPTER
THREE

AT ABOUT SIX o'clock of the same day, Lunex received assay results on the most recent Mountain Lake drill cores. Manetti and Ransom, both in a state of euphoric shock, were hard at work on the media release,

"The street will accuse us of doing a Bre-X," said Ransom, handing his marked-up draft to Manetti.

"So will our own directors," replied Manetti. "Ann's arranging a telephone meeting of the Board for seven o'clock. I assume she told you."

"Yes, I'll be there. The directors who don't accuse us of smoking something will accuse us of salting something. If Fennell had the hots for us before, what will he do when we report these results?"

"We're in play for sure," agreed Manetti.

"Truth be told, I'm just as glad. We've been looking over our shoulder for the last year, waiting for Noramet to take a run at us, waiting for the shoe to drop, so let it drop."

"I said as much to Graydon this morning, but I was whistling past the graveyard. What do you know that I don't?"

"Nothing ... but we've reviewed all our options. So, let the war games stop and the war begin."

"*Options?* Let's face it, Warren, all we've got is a faint hope that Laurentian Mining will enter the lists as our white knight."

"Okay, option ... *singular.*"

"Yes, and a very faint option. I think Alastair Drake wants us, but why would the Laurentian Board want to tangle with big Noramet?"

"Look at these assay results," protested Ransom. "The potential of this goldfield makes my head spin. Surely Drake will be able to sell his Board."

Manetti shrugged. "We live in hope, but frankly, I don't see how Alastair will be able to convince his Board to forgo a good cash offer for their Lunex shares. Even if he succeeds—even if the Laurentian directors elect to participate in Mountain Lake—why wouldn't they just tender their Lunex shares for Noramet shares and go along for the ride as a Noramet shareholder? Whether Noramet or Lunex develops Mountain Lake is of little import to Laurentian. Either way, they'll reap the rewards of Mountain Lake."

"I hope you're underestimating both Drake *and* his Board."

"So do I, but if I were a Laurentian director, I'd say the only choice is between tendering their Lunex shares for Noramet cash or tendering their Lunex shares for Noramet shares. Frankly, I can't see them launching a counter-bid to a Noramet takeover bid. Why would they want to get into a pissing contest with Noramet?"

"To win the prize? To get control of Mountain Lake? To keep the Lunex team on the job?"

"We're the best, but let's not delude ourselves that we're the one and only. Let's face facts! Noramet could complete the exploration work at Mountain Lake and develop the orebody."

"So, you think we're toast."

"I think we need a miracle. However, Yogi says it ain't over 'til it's over, so let's go nine innings and pray for a miracle. Quite apart from the Laurentian Board, the Laurentian management team will be supporting a Noramet bid. Take Ross Macdonald, for example. Unless I miss my guess, he'll be slavering at the prospect of a windfall gain. It would be great for the Laurentian balance sheet, great for the Laurentian share price, great for Macdonald's annual bonus, and great for Macdonald's stock options."

"*Ross Macdonald!*" Ransom sneered the name. "I'm astonished Laurentian got saddled with a prick like Ross Macdonald in the first place. I'm astonished he became COO, and I'm astonished he's still there. Sooner or later, good companies always slough off bad people."

"I don't know about that," grinned Manetti. "You're still here."

"Yes, waiting patiently for Lunex to slough you off. From what I hear on the grapevine, Macdonald's roundly disliked over there. They think he's a real jerk."

"I wonder if he knows or cares."

"I suspect he knows, and I doubt he cares! He's a conceited bastard."

"Warren, old friend, maybe you and I are roundly disliked at Lunex. Who would dare tell us that we're a couple of jerks?"

"Ann Stevenson, for starters."

"You're right there," chuckled Manetti. "However, if either you or I were in Macdonald's shoes, I dare say we too would be slavering at the prospect of a windfall gain. Anyway, Laurentian's our only hope, and Alastair is the only possible miracle worker. So pray for the miracle!"

"I've been praying. Believe me." Ransom shrugged. "What the hell! If we lose, we lose! The worst-case scenario ain't all that bad. I mean, our group ends up tendering to the Noramet bid, we all make millions, and we all retire rich."

"This isn't about *rich,* and you know it. I'm already rich, and so are you. Money will be no consolation for losing Mountain Lake, and even if it were, who wants to retire? I'm old enough to think of retirement, but you're too young to retire. You're still a kid."

"A kid of fifty-four. Haven't you heard of *Freedom Fifty-Five?*"

"What would you do if you retired?"

"Stop working."

"Bugger off! I'm not ready, and neither are you. If Noramet bags Lunex, we'll start another company ... but we'll sure as hell go down fighting before we lose this one."

"I've been waiting to hear some fighting words from you. I know that Noramet's your Moby Dick, and I know why, but believe me when I tell you that I hate Fennell a thousand times more than you do."

"That's a tall claim. I know you joined Noramet not long after I left, but you never did tell me why you quit."

"You offered me a job."

"You came looking for a job, as I recall, so you traded a secure position with Noramet for a flier with me. When you joined Lunex, all I could offer you was share options. Back then, we didn't have a corporate pot to piss in. Anyway, Warren, why you left Noramet is none of my business. Damn Fennell! He thinks he can sit on his fat ass and control North American gold mining from his fat-ass Wall Street office."

"Trouble is, he can, and he does," replied Ransom.

Manetti made a few more revisions to the release and handed it back to Ransom. "Are you okay with those changes?"

Ransom read the annotations and nodded.

"Call the stock exchanges first thing in the morning and co-ordinate with them. They'll want to postpone trading until this hot news has been well and truly broadcast. As you say, the street will accuse us of doing a Bre-X."

CHAPTER
FOUR

"HERE'S NEWS!" IT was Wednesday morning, just shy of nine o'clock, as Ross Macdonald burst into Alastair Drake's office.

Drake looked displeased at the interruption. "Come in, since you're in," he said, setting aside his file. "Where's Lorraine?"

"Your guard dog wasn't barring the door, so I'm announcing myself. Lunex has reported blockbuster drilling results from their Mountain Lake camp. Treasury tells me the TSX has postponed trading until ten-thirty. I got this wire report from Treasury, but I haven't yet seen the actual media release."

Without replying, Drake handed him a copy of the Lunex release, and without pausing, Macdonald snatched up the telephone on Drake's desk and called through to his secretary. "I'm looking for a media release from Lunex. Tell those dozy bastards in Public Affairs that I expect to get important news while it's still news." He slammed the receiver and began to read the text.

"She could have heard you without the telephone," said Drake. "Tell me, do you often refer to our esteemed colleagues as *dozy bastards?*"

"Not the esteemed ones," said Macdonald, without looking up.

"I think we have an excellent Public Affairs group. I recruited them myself."

Macdonald finished his perusal and handed the release back to Drake. "If they're so damn good, why wasn't that release on my desk when I arrived this morning? Why are they asleep at the switch? If the president of the company isn't kept informed, then who the hell is?"

"The CEO, I guess."

"That goes without saying, but this release should have been on my desk too … first thing this morning. When did Public Affairs notify you?"

"Actually, I notified Public Affairs. Rocco Manetti briefed the Lunex directors yesterday evening, and Warren Ransom faxed the release to me about an hour ago."

"Thanks for keeping me in the loop."

"Sorry, Ross, it slipped my mind. I guess I'm just another one of those dozy bastards who's trying to keep you in the dark."

"This news will put Lunex into play for sure," said Macdonald, trying to ignore the barb and mask his anger.

"I'm sorry to say it will."

"I'm not a bit sorry. With all that Lunex stock in our portfolio, Laurentian stands to make a killing. Let the auction begin, I say."

"Leave Rocco alone, I say. Let him grow Lunex, I say."

"Bugger Manetti! A juicy takeover premium for our Lunex shares is just what our balance sheet needs."

Drake shrugged. "I'm sorry for Rocco nonetheless. He stands to lose his company."

"He also stands to make a personal fortune. I wonder how long the Lunex lads have been privy to this news?"

"They got the assay results late yesterday afternoon."

"Yes. Confirming what they already knew."

"Let me ask you something, Ross. Do you ever engage in insider trading?"

"No, it's too risky."

"*Risky?* What about *unethical?* What about *illegal?* In any event, the *Lunex lads* don't engage in insider trading either."

"None to speak of, eh? No, I'm sure you're right. The TSX'll be checking the trading records eight ways against the centre, so as I say, it would be too risky."

"I'd prefer to think they act on principle."

"I'm sure they do. The principle of not getting caught. Nevertheless, Manetti must have been tempted. I know I'd have been tempted."

"I'll pretend I didn't hear that."

"Come on, Alastair, you've been around a long time, and so have I. You must have made a few dollars on inside information over the years. I know I have."

"I'll also pretend I didn't hear that."

"Don't worry, it happened in the U.K., and it happened many years ago … before I joined Laurentian and before the Girl Guides seized control of the Ontario Securities Commission. Way back then, you could buy and sell stock without dropping your pants in public. I see I've scandalized you, so I'd better go."

"Please do!" Drake glanced at a chart on his desk. "I see you're chairing an Annual Plan Meeting … and that it started five minutes ago. They may have started without you."

"I hope not, for their sake. Would Your Holiness like to address the group today? Perhaps a homily on insider trading?"

"No, but I'd like to join the group for lunch. Let me know when you break."

Macdonald left Drake's office and went straight to the boardroom, where a dozen or more Laurentian officers were assembled and waiting—division officers summoned from the far reaches of Laurentian's mining empire—together with a few head office denizens of various disciplines. The out-of-towners disliked and dreaded

Black Angus and his meetings from hell, almost as much as they disliked and dreaded his flying visits to their mining operations. The head office people disliked Black Angus too, but were inured to him and his meetings from hell.

Black Angus wasn't a friendly nickname. *Black* was aimed at Macdonald's ugly personality, *Angus* at his beefy physique—a physique that would have been presentable in most wrestling rings.

Although no one dared call him Black Angus to his face, Macdonald knew they called him that behind his back, and he rather fancied the nickname. He liked being disliked. He liked firing people and found it less complicated to do so when the terminator and the terminated harboured mutual antipathy. He would have terminated many more people over the years had Drake not repeatedly overruled him.

Without bothering to greet or even acknowledge the assembled group, Macdonald went straight to the sideboard and poured himself a cup of coffee. Then he took the chairman's place at the head of the boardroom table and called for the first presenter.

Anyone who had the misfortune to be a presenter at a Black Angus meeting knew in advance that he was in for a rough ride. He was steeled to the fact that Macdonald would make challenging and sarcastic interjections, intended to throw him off-stride and disrupt the flow of his presentation. That was Macdonald's style—except with women, of whom there were few at Laurentian. Whenever a female presenter appeared at a Black Angus meeting, Macdonald patronized her by being dismissively and excessively courteous.

Black Angus was a master at ragging his subordinates. He enjoyed putting them on the defensive and keeping them there. He thought of it as *testing their mettle*. He thought of Laurentian as an army of conscripts rather than a college of professionals, and he regarded himself as the quintessential Roman general. The fact that Drake was more of a dean than a general was, in Macdonald's view, a sign of weak management. When Drake was no longer there to protect the troops, Macdonald fully intended to impose military discipline by decimating the ranks. He meant what he was fond of saying: "*No one owns his job*" and "*Here today but don't count on tomorrow.*"

Ruthless he was, but talented too—an excellent mind driven by a strong work ethic. He acquired his ruthlessness (among other personality disorders) during, and as a result of, an underprivileged childhood in Scotland. As he had brawled his way out of the slums of Glasgow, so had he brawled his way to the top of Laurentian. The rungs of Laurentian's corporate ladder were caked with the gore of his face-trodden victims, most of them better men than he. Now there was just one more rung to go: the top rung—a rung which he expected to attain by succession rather than aggression.

Although one might have expected a kid from the Glasgow slums to be imbued with egalitarian instincts, Macdonald was an elitist through and through. Although his chosen elite was rather down-market—limited as it was to businessmen—it was certainly not down-at-the-heels, and even detractors of the capitalist system will concede that the elite of Corporate North America rank slightly higher on the social scale than the slum-dwellers of Glasgow.

Was Macdonald a genuine elitist or a fake elitist in flight from his squalid origins? That's a question for psychiatrists, but you don't have to be a shrink to know when someone needs one, and his subordinates all knew that Black Angus was in urgent need of counselling.

Because of his elitism, and because of his narrow and narrow-minded focus on himself and his own career, Macdonald seldom mingled with Laurentian officers who were junior in rank to him, a cohort which now included everyone except Alastair Drake. They could neither advance nor hinder his career—or so he thought—and he had no interest in advancing their careers.

It should be noted here that Macdonald was even-handed in his selfish disregard for others. Not only did he turn his back on his colleagues, he also ignored the folks back home in Glasgow—a source of resentment and disappointment to his impoverished parents and impecunious siblings. They had expected *their Ross*—their successful and affluent Ross—to remember them in times of need. However, they soon learned that *their Ross* was much too busy to remember them in times of need, or indeed, in any other times. He never went back, or looked back, to Glasgow. He sloughed off Glasgow and his family as easily and naturally as a snake sloughs off its skin, although he never managed to slough off his Scottish burr. He didn't even return for the funerals of his parents, and being a very busy businessman, he forgot to remember requests for a rateable contribution to the funeral expenses. To be fair, it should be noted that he had his secretary send extravagant floral tributes to both funerals, although, as Laurentian's Assistant Comptroller noted—quietly and to himself alone—Macdonald charged those flowers to the company. Busy businessmen, like busy politicians, can't allow themselves to get bogged down in petty matters of petty cash.

The tension-filled Black Angus meeting continued non-stop until twelve-thirty, by which time everyone was tired, hungry, dejected of spirit, and distended of bladder.

"We'll break for lunch and resume at one o'clock sharp," growled Macdonald. "We're running late, so I hope the afternoon presenters will be more focussed than the ones we've heard so far."

A flash fire couldn't have cleared the place faster. The group moved *en masse* from boardroom to bathroom to buffet. Black Angus was giving them a mingy half hour, little enough time to eat and no time to escape the building for a brief stroll. Since out-of-towners would be rushing to catch homebound flights when this meeting from hell ended, there would be no time to purchase items which wives had requisitioned—items readily available in Toronto but unattainable in remote mining communities. Mining wives resented Black Angus every bit as much as did their husbands.

Except for Macdonald, who was welcomed for his absence, the group foregathered in the dining room for a brief but pleasant social interlude, which was the only pleasant part of an unpleasant day. Alastair Drake joined the group for lunch and made a point of chatting with each and every one of the out-of-towners. His genuine interest in Laurentian employees, as individuals, had engendered loyalty and an *esprit de corps* throughout the organization—loyalty and *esprit de corps* that Macdonald had managed to impair but not destroy.

It was downright astonishing to most Laurentian people that the successor-apparent to the well-liked and respected Drake was the disliked and disrespected Macdonald. Employees who were in a position to take early retirement were planning to do just that, if and when Black Angus took the helm.

For his part, Macdonald went straight from the boardroom to his office and despatched his secretary to fetch him lunch from the buffet. Then he began sorting through his messages, several prolix voice-mails, a fistful of e-mails, and half a dozen telephone slips. It was all business as usual, except for one telephone call from a Bill Graydon, who had left his telephone number but no message.

When his secretary returned with lunch, he thrust the telephone slip at her. "Who's Graydon and what does he want?"

"I don't know, Mr. Macdonald."

"Why didn't you ask?"

"I did, but he wouldn't leave a message."

Macdonald released a dissatisfied grunt and began to shovel food into his face. Then he waved his fork in her general direction, his mouth chock-full of partially masticated lunch. "The only Graydon I can think of is an investment banker. I think he may be the head guy at Thorne Sullivan … something like that." He paused to swallow, which he managed with some difficulty and a little choking. "He's a slimy bastard, if he's the one I'm thinking of. Check that phone number against Thorne Sullivan."

She left and returned shortly to confirm his guess, whereupon he dismissed her with another impatient wave of the fork.

As he wolfed his lunch, Macdonald eyed the mystery telephone slip with suspicion, trying to divine the reason for the call. He knew who Graydon was but couldn't guess what Graydon wanted. Laurentian had never retained Thorne Sullivan, and if Graydon was trying to drum up business, he'd be telephoning Drake. Having cleaned his plate, he leaned back and belched loudly. Then he belched again and punched in the telephone number.

"Graydon here."

"Ross Macdonald."

"Ross! Thanks for getting back to me." Apparently Ross was Graydon's long-lost buddy. "You may recall we met briefly in Ottawa, a couple of months ago, at a Mining Association reception."

Macdonald didn't remember but said he did.

"Ross, I'm calling on a very sensitive matter, too sensitive to discuss on the telephone. Could we arrange a meeting?"

"I guess we could. Sounds all *cloak and dagger*. Can you give me a hint?"

"I'd rather talk face-to-face. Could we get together for lunch or dinner some time soon?"

"I guess we could. I have to admit you've got me curious."

"Do you have any time available tomorrow?"

"Thursday? No, I'm in New York tomorrow, and I've booked off Friday to get a head start on the Labour Day weekend." He paused, and then apparently felt obliged to justify his truancy. "I haven't had a vacation all summer."

"I certainly don't want to interfere with your long weekend, especially since I'm planning to take Friday off too. However, I'd really like to talk to you this week, if at all possible."

"I guess I could see you tonight, if it's urgent."

"Perfect! I'll arrange for a private room at the Toronto Club. Is six thirty okay for you?"

"Sure, six thirty's fine. Private room? This *is* cloak and dagger. Shall I wear my Sherlock Holmes' cap?"

Graydon responded with a forced laugh. "When I have a chance to tell you what this is about, I hope you'll forgive the cloak and dagger trappings. In the meantime, please keep this conversation in strict confidence."

CHAPTER
FIVE

MANETTI'S INTERCOM BUZZED. "Yes, Ann?"

"There's someone at reception wants to see you."

Manetti glanced at his day timer for Wednesday, August 28. "I don't have any appointments, and I'm in a meeting with Warren."

"I know that, Rocco, but Irene can't get rid of him and neither can I. He's been drinking."

"At ten in the morning? Must be a freelance prospector, down on his luck. What's his name?"

"He won't say. All he'll say is '*Tell Rocco his old hockey buddy is here.*' Do you have an old hockey buddy who's a drunk?"

"I'm afraid I do. Does the name Pat O'Malley mean anything to you?"

"No."

"He used to play for the Detroit Red Wings, back in the seventies and eighties. Damn good defenceman."

"I was in public school back in the seventies."

"Yes, I guess you were. Didn't you watch hockey?"

"No, and I still don't. I wish I could say the same for my husband. Anyway, will you come out and get rid of him?"

"Okay, I'll see him in a few minutes. Put him in the conference room and keep him happy 'til I get there."

"He's half drunk."

"Then you won't have any trouble keeping him happy. Charm the pants off him."

"He's not my type."

"*His* pants, not yours; I won't be long."

"I'm going to leave the door open, that's for sure."

"You always get the last word, don't you!"

"Yes."

Manetti hung up, shaking his head. "Sorry, Warren, an unexpected visitor. Do you remember a hockey star of yesteryear named O'Malley? Pat O'Malley?"

"Afraid not."

"Neither does Ann. So much for our national game."

"You forget I'm a Brit. Soccer's my game."

"Well then, I won't introduce you. Paddy wasn't quite a star, but he was good … better than a journeyman. Now he's a drunk. Believe it or not, I used to be a good hockey player in my youth."

"Good enough to turn professional?"

"That I'll never know. Paddy told me I blew my chances by going to college, and he's probably right."

In a few minutes, Manetti left Ransom and strode down the corridor to the conference room. True to her word, Ann had left the door open, and Manetti paused outside to eavesdrop. O'Malley was regaling his captive audience with anecdotes about the NHL, and she was feigning interest in the slurred monologue. Manetti knocked on the open door.

"Paddy O'Malley, we meet again … and so soon. I see you've met Mrs. Stevenson, our chatelaine. So, you'd probably prefer that she stays and I leave."

Ann Stevenson was relieved to get her cue. "I really must be off, Dr. Manetti. Mr. O'Malley has been telling me some fascinating stories about his hockey career."

"Paddy was one of the best."

"I'm sure he was." She moved to the doorway. "Well then, I'll have coffee sent in, shall I? It's been very nice meeting you, Mr. O'Malley."

O'Malley stumbled to his feet. "Same here, Annie! Same here, eh?"

Manetti closed the door behind her, and O'Malley subsided into his chair, somewhat involuntarily. "Nice legs!" he smirked. "Tell me, *Doctor* Manetti, what's *chatelaine* mean?"

"Mistress of the castle."

"She's your mistress?"

"She's nobody's mistress, Paddy. She's Mr. Stevenson's wife. I trust my cheque didn't bounce."

"No! Good as gold!"

"And I trust you paid off the loan shark."

"Sure! Sure!"

"Well then, do you mind telling me why you're here?"

"I've come about my booster pension."

"Your *what?*"

"It's not *what*, Rocco, it's *who*. It's *you*, Rocco. You're my booster pension."

"I don't like the sound of this, so let's have it, straight and simple. No obfuscations."

"Why don'tcha speak English, eh?"

"No double talk! *Capisce?*"

"Okay, Rocco, no double talk and no obfuck ... whatever-you-said." O'Malley's hands suddenly began shaking, and he started mopping his brow. "Can we go somewhere and get a drink?"

"No, we can't. The bars aren't open, and I'm busy." He studied O'Malley's sweating face for a moment and then opened one of the teak wall cabinets, which discreetly housed a small bar. He filled a tumbler with Scotch, added ice, and handed it over. "Okay, now what's on your mind?"

O'Malley cradled the tumbler in both of his shaking hands, and then took a generous slug, taking care not to spill any of the precious liquid. He stared lovingly into the depths of the glass before taking a second infusion. Manetti felt both disgusted and sad as he watched the alcohol revive the alcoholic. "So, what's on your mind? I haven't got much time."

There was a knock at the door, followed by a young woman who left a tray of coffee. O'Malley drained his glass and handed it back for a refill. Manetti set the glass aside and handed him the bottle. "It's yours, compliments of Lunex, but drink it later. It's coffee time."

Waving away the proffered coffee, O'Malley pulled the cork from the bottle and took a long swig. Then he peered admiringly at the label, admiration verging on worship. "*Balvenie*... This is good stuff." He was awestruck, a diner magically transported from the Golden Arches to Maximes. "I'm gonna get me some *Balvenie* for sure."

Manetti poured himself a cup of coffee and then tapped his watch.

"Okay, Rocco, you're in a hurry, so here goes." O'Malley fished a photograph from his jacket and slid it across the table. "I brought along a picher for your family album."

Manetti looked at the photograph and then calmly slid it back. "That proves nothing."

"The police might think different, after I've done my show and tell."

"The police might wonder why you've been sitting on it for forty years."

"I thought of that one, Rocco." O'Malley tapped his forehead. "I decided you must have threatened to kill me, if I didn't keep my mouth shut, so I was afraid. Don't you remember threatenin' to kill me? I think they call it *intimidation*. Poor little me, eh? I was intimidated. Anyway, it's preyed on my conscious all these years. So, now I'm ready to do the right thing." He smirked and took a pull from the bottle. "I saw that on TV. Some asshole says, '*It preyed on my conscious all these years, so now I'm ready to do the right thing.*' I figured that was a good line for Pat O'Malley to remember."

"That's a great line, but the word you want is '*conscience*'."

"Whatever! It's almost true, you know. I mean, you didn't threaten to kill me, but I figger you probably would have if you'd known I was on to you ... so it's almost true. If I was in your shoes, I'd have threatened to kill me ... so it's almost true. It's as good as true, you might say."

"All you've got is a grainy photograph."

"I got more than one, Rocco. More than one. If a picher's worth a thousand words, then I figger I got a whole book."

"How much do you want, O'Malley?"

"Not much, Rocco, not much; after all, we're old hockey buddies, eh?"

"How much?"

"Well, I played hockey in the days before the big salaries, and let's face it, I never made the All-Star Team."

"Skip the shilly-shallying. You're here to blackmail me, so how much do you want for the photographs?"

"I was thinkin' along the lines of two grand a month. That's only twenty-four grand a year." O'Malley stole a glance at his prospective benefactor, but Manetti remained stone-faced. "Hell, Rocco, from what I read in the papers, you guys are swimmin' in money. Hell, two grand a month is chump change to a minin' magnet like you."

"I'm a magnet all right, a magnet for trouble." For a long minute, Manetti tilted his chair and stared at the ceiling. Then he tilted back.. "So, for *twenty-four grand a year*, you hand over all the photographs and any other evidence."

O'Malley shifted in his chair. "I figger I should hang on to a couple of pichers ... just for insurance. I trust you, Rocco, but—"

"No *buts*!" interrupted Manetti. "No *buts*! What would happen to the *insurance photographs* when you die?"

"I hadn't thought of that one. How be I leave them in a sealed envelope addressed to you?"

"Yes, that would be a clear enough road map for the police. Great idea!"

"Hell, Rocco, them pichers don't prove nothin'."

"Then why did you take them?"

"I mean, they don't prove nothin' without my show-and-tell, eh?"

"They prove plenty; that's why you took them."

"Relax, Rocco! I'm expectin' to be around for a few more years. We've got lots of time to cover your ass."

"Don't count on it, not the way you're boozing. In any event, what if I die before you do?"

"Hadn't thought of that one either. I guess you'd want to remember me in your will."

"And if I didn't?"

"Well, I guess I'd have to sell the pichers I had to the highest bidder. I bet Pierrette would pay plenty to keep that skeleton in the closet. I bet she would, eh?"

"It'd be easy to blackmail my widow, wouldn't it? With me gone, you'd probably blackmail her whether or not I took care of you in my will."

"No way! I'm not a crook! You can trust me, Rocco."

"Since when do *trust* and *blackmail* go hand-in-hand? I want *all* the photographs, and *all* the other evidence, or there's no deal. *Capisce?* If you keep even *one* insurance photograph, you might as well keep them all. I'll cover you by arranging for an annuity: a $24,000 annuity on your life, so we won't have to *trust* each other. I won't be able to renege on our deal, and you won't need any insurance photographs."

O'Malley shrugged. "I don't care how I get the money, just so long as I get it." Then his face clouded. "But wouldn't I have to pay income tax, like I do on my NHL pension? Hell, it's the income tax that's keepin' me poor."

"Join the club; it's the Canadian way ... our patriotic vow of perpetual poverty."

"You got that right! Them French fries in Ottawa piss it away faster than we can make it. Look, why don'tcha just slip me two grand every month? Keep it simple, eh?"

"Because, O'Malley, *old hockey buddy-turned-blackmailer*, I want to be quit of you, once and for all. I'll arrange for a $36,000 annuity. The extra twelve thousand will offset your income tax. I presume you'll pay the tax."

"Sure! Sure! I always say you shouldn't cheat the guvermint just 'cause the guvermint cheats you." O'Malley grinned in self-appreciation and rewarded himself with a pull on the bottle. "I figger I pay enough taxes just on this stuff. Do you know how much tax we pay on booze? It's practically all tax. Anyway, I've got an accountant who does my income tax forms, and I pay whatever he tells me to pay. I used to be a good client, back in my playin' days, but he still looks after me. Don't charge me much, but I guess there's not much to charge me for. He'll be surprised to find out about this annuity thing."

"So will some accountants around here. Look, I haven't figured out exactly how to book this. I guess the annuity could be payment for the sale of mining claims."

"What minin' claims?" O'Malley was suspicious.

"You may well ask. Maybe I registered certain mining claims in my name but am holding an undivided one-half interest in trust for you. Maybe you used to do some prospecting in your younger days. Maybe you want me to buy you out."

O'Malley's face lit up in a gap-toothed grin. "Sure, Rocco, I remember them claims. You're gonna buy me out, right?"

"Right. You'll be receiving an assignment agreement some time in the next couple of weeks. Sign it and send it back to me. Do you have a lawyer?"

"Sort of, I guess. Sammy Linzner used to be my lawyer and my agent, back in my NHL days. I guess he's still my lawyer 'cause he does a will for me every now and then. He never charges me nothin', so I don't know how good a lawyer he is."

"Well, don't—I repeat, *don't*—consult him about this. If you have any questions, call me and I'll explain it. *Don't* consult your accountant either. In fact, don't consult *anyone*. It'll be a fictitious paper trail to back up the annuity. That's all it'll be, and I don't want anyone nosing around. You can go to jail for extortion too. *Capisce?*"

"Sure! Sure!"

"Good! Now that we're partners in crime, I have a question. Once we've got the paperwork done and you've got the annuity, how do I know you'll deliver all the evidence and keep your mouth shut? Convince me!"

O'Malley paused to consider his answer and to take another slug of Scotch. "I've kept my trap shut all these years … free, *gratis*, for nothin'. Now you're payin' me to keep my trap shut. Also, I wouldn't double-cross an old hockey buddy."

"Those are good answers, but I'll give you a better one." Manetti moved around the table and gripped the back of O'Malley's neck. "As long as you honour our little deal, you have nothing to fear from me. Double-cross me and you do." He tightened his grip. "And just in case I predecease you, I'll make arrangements to enforce our little deal after I'm gone."

O'Malley knocked Manetti's arms aside. "Tough talk, but it don't scare me. For starters, I'm a helluva lot bigger than you."

Manetti gripped O'Malley's neck again. "Do you want to try me on for size? Like right now?"

Again, O'Malley broke Manetti's grip. "If we're partners, you should trust me, eh? You shouldn't be goin' around threatenin' me."

Manetti prodded O'Malley roughly. "We're not *partners*, O'Malley. You're a blackmailer, and I'm your mark. Let's get the arrangements crystal clear so nobody gets seriously hurt." He returned to his chair. "A couple of minutes ago, you said *I'd have threatened to kill you if I'd known about the photographs.* You're dead right there! So, don't even think of double-crossing me or you're dead meat. *Capisce?*"

"You can trust me without no threats." O'Malley was sullen. "So, when do I get my money?"

"It'll probably take two or three weeks to get the paperwork in place. Here, write your address and telephone number on this pad."

O'Malley completed the assignment with some difficulty. "Look, Rocco, I'm a little short, so I was hopin' we could start the payments right away."

"Where have I heard this before?"

"You know what I did with the five grand—"

"And now you need some upfront money."

Upfront money sounded businesslike to O'Malley, so he seized on it. "That's it, Rocco, I need some upfront money. I mean the Labour Day weekend's comin' up, and the banks will be closed."

"This is only Wednesday. The banks will be open for three days, and the cash machines are always open. Anyway, I'm tied up today, and I'm flying up north in the morning. I won't be back until Tuesday afternoon, so the best I can do is Tuesday evening. Two thousand dollars Tuesday evening."

O'Malley shifted uneasily. "I'll level with you, Rocco, I'm flat broke. I need some cash right now, like today."

Manetti opened his billfold and peeled off four fifty-dollar bills. "I guess you think I'm your cash machine."

"Thanks, Rocco. I really appreciate it, eh?"

"So, I'll deliver $1,800 on Tuesday evening. Where do we meet?"

O'Malley shrugged. "Don't matter to me. Look, why don'tcha leave it here. I could drop by Tuesday afternoon and pick it up from Annie."

"You haven't been listening, O'Malley. I want quit of you, once and for all. I don't want you coming around here again. *Ever again!* You're not welcome here."

O'Malley looked sad rather than insulted, realizing that his fantasy-romance with Ann Stevenson was being nipped in the bud. Manetti consulted his diary. "I spoke too soon. Pierrette and I have tickets for Soulpepper next Tuesday. What about Wednesday?"

"*Wednesday!* My back's against the wall, Rocco. A brick wall."

"More loan sharks?"

"Let's just say I can't wait 'til next Wednesday."

"And let's just say I'm too busy to deal with a blackmailer at the drop of a hat. I guess you should have started shaking me down sooner."

"C'mon, Rocco, don't take it personal-like. Couldn't you just write me a cheque like you did on Monday?"

"Definitely not! I'm not about to set up a paper trail for the police. If you need the money before Wednesday, you can take Pierrette to Soulpepper on Tuesday evening. I'll send an envelope with her."

"What's Soulpepper?"

"A theatre."

"Movies?"

"Plays."

Panic filled O'Malley's face. "No way, Rocco! That's not my thing." He held both palms forward in a gesture of rejection. "No way I'm goin' to that Soulpepper place. No way!"

"Too bad! Pierette would love to meet you again. All the Sudbury girls remember their hockey hero ... the great O'Malley."

"Get off it! Pierrette wouldn't remember me."

"She talks of little else. However, if you don't want to take Pierrette, I could give the tickets to Ann Stevenson. How would that suit you?"

"Great!" responded O'Malley with an inebriated grin. "But would we have to go to that theatre thing? I mean, she could bring the money up to my place." He pointed to his shabby jacket. "I mean, I can't go to no theatre in this, eh? This is about all I got."

Manetti pointed to his own plaid shirt. "I go in this."

Through the alcoholic haze, O'Malley suddenly realized that Manetti had been mocking him, and his anger flared. "Bullshit! Bullshit you do! I've seen you in the newspapers. You in a tux, Pierrette in a fancy gown. You think you're one of them society assholes, but all you really are is a jumped-up wop from Copper Cliff and don't forget it ... and don't go puttin' me down."

"*Wop* is a fighting word, O'Malley, so don't use it again ... unless you're looking for a fight."

"What a classy girl like Pierrette Legault saw in you is a mystery to me, and everybody else in Sudbury. Now you're one of them society assholes who have the best seats in every arena in the league. They come late, leave early, and don't pay attention to the game—specially the women. And if they know you, they're too stuck up to come 'round after the game and say hello."

"The best I can do is Tuesday evening, after the play. Take it or leave it."

"Okay, *Doctor Society Big Shot*, I'll see you Tuesday after your Soulpepper thing."

"The question is *where?* I'll be coming from the Distillery District, probably around ten o'clock. So, where do you want to meet?"

"Don't matter," replied O'Malley, still angry.

Manetti thought for a moment and then drew a quick sketch on a note pad. "Go to this parking lot on Queen's Quay, and park somewhere in the open where I can find you. Do you know the place?"

O'Malley looked at the map and nodded.

"Good! What are you driving?"

"A 1990 Escort, dark blue." O'Malley looked embarrassed. "I told you I was broke."

Manetti stood up, indicating that the interview was over. "Get there by ten, because I'm not going to hang around waiting."

O'Malley lurched to his feet, not forgetting to take the half empty bottle. Manetti rummaged in a wall cabinet and produced a large padded envelope. "Here, you'd better carry the booze in this."

He escorted him to the elevator lobby, and just before the elevator arrived, made direct eye contact. "Don't even *think* of double-crossing me, O'Malley. Your life depends on keeping your mouth shut, so keep it shut. *Tightly* shut."

Although he had been cool under fire, Manetti was badly shaken by this sinister turn of events. He returned to the conference room to calm his nerves and collect his thoughts, but he succeeded in doing neither. As if in a nightmare, he was haunted by jumbled and stormy memories, and then his mind drifted to calmer waters: his first encounters with Pierrette.

Their first meeting had been an inauspicious beginning to a life-long romance—a beginning born of a chance encounter between him and Pierrette's brother Michel. Manetti and Pierrette were both in first year at Queen's University, returning to school after Christmas holidays, trudging stoically through a wind-whipped snowstorm. She was being escorted by her brother, a person whom Manetti thoroughly disliked and who in turn thoroughly disliked Manetti. However, since all three were plodding heads bent against the elements, neither man spotted the other until it was too late, and since the antagonists couldn't avoid each other, they were reluctantly forced to acknowledge each other. He remembered that encounter vividly, as if it had occurred yesterday.

"Hello, Legault, I wouldn't expect to find you around here."

"Just passing through, Manetti. You're playing for Queen's, I hear. Too bad the NHL doesn't scout college kids."

"Right. I guess I'll have to do something else for a living."

"Yeah, sooner or later, you'll have to quit school and face the real world."

"Like you?"

"Yeah, a grownup doing grownup work—"

"At one of his daddy's companies."

"Sneer now, Manetti, but you're talking to the future CEO of Legault Industries. We're hiring at the warehouse, if you want a real job."

"Thanks anyway. I have other career plans."

"At Inco's smelter? Like your old man? Good idea! Keep it in the family."

"Career counseling from a high-school dropout! What next?"

"Best move I ever made! Wish I'd quit school years ago."

"So do the schools." Manetti had then stepped around Legault and extended his gloved hand to the girl whom Legault was not about to introduce. "We haven't met. My name's Rocco Manetti."

"I'm Michel's sister, Pierrette," she had replied, looking very ill-at-ease as she extended her right mitten.

"Pierrette's my twin sister. I look after her. I look out for her."

Pointedly ignoring Legault, Manetti spoke directly to Pierrette. "You have my sympathy."

It was inevitable that Pierrette Legault and Rocco Manetti would meet again, and that inevitable meeting had occurred a few days later, more or less on purpose.

Manetti greeted her enthusiastically. "Hello again! Glad you survived the storm."

"I've been on the lookout for you," she replied, and then blushed. "I mean, I want to apologize for Michel ... the way he acted last Sunday. He was very rude."

"So was I."

"Yes, you were, but I can't apologize for you."

"Then I'll apologize for myself. It must have been embarrassing for you."

"It was awkward, I'm curious to know why you two dislike each other so much."

"That's a fair question, but I don't know the answer. Perhaps you could call it blood chemistry; he's a little rich for my blood, and I'm a little poor for his. Whatever the reason, we've never been best friends and that's not likely to change. I knew Michel had a sister, and I've seen you around Sudbury occasionally, but we've never met before. Where did you go to school?"

"I was sent away to the Ursulines in Quebec. My grandmother thought she was grooming me for Quebec City society. That's where the Legault clan holds court."

"Your father holds a rather big court in Sudbury."

"Yes, he's the Legault rebel."

"Not much Quebec City society around Queen's."

"Exactly! I'm a rebel too. My grandmother's still sulking that I gave a pass to Laval, but my mother's okay with Queen's ... mainly because she doesn't much like my grandmother. Anyway, here I am: a good Catholic girl at Presbyterian Queen's. What about you?"

"I suppose I'm a bad Catholic boy at Presbyterian Queen's."

"Are you a bad Catholic or a bad boy?"

"My mother thinks I'm a bad Catholic."

"Are you a bad boy as well?"

"I guess that depends on whom you ask."

"Whom should I ask?"

"Not your brother."

She laughed. "No, definitely not Michel! I'll ask your mother. Why did you choose Queen's?"

"I was being groomed for the mine, mill, and smelter society, but scholarships funded my escape. I'm a rebel too."

"You're making fun of me."

"No, just answering your question. Now it's my turn. What's your course?"

"Engineering."

"Mmm... That's an odd choice."

"For a girl, you mean."

"I didn't say that."

"I was just finishing your sentence. Michel also thinks it's an odd choice for a girl. So, you and Michel agree on something."

"Are you planning a career in engineering?"

"I don't know. I'll probably join Legault Industries. Daddy's little girl ... that's what you're thinking."

"There you go again, trying to read my mind."

"No, I was reading your expression. You should never play poker. Anyway, believe it or not, it's a curse having a rich father."

"Cry me a river!"

"Michel thinks you're Il Diablo, but maybe he's been unfair."

"Definitely unfair! Based on my dealings with your brother, I've grown up thinking you must be a witch. Maybe I've been unfair."

"Definitely unfair."

"It appears that our damaged reputations need repair. Can we meet for coffee some time? I'll do my level best to convince you I'm not Il Diablo, and you can bewitch me."

"Michel would kill me. You don't know my brother."

"Unfortunately, I do. I promise not to tell him."

"He'd find out."

"Kingston's a long way from Sudbury. May I call you?"

"Yes, I guess so, but first there's something I need to know. You and Michel dislike each other..."

"You know that already."

"Yes, but that's my problem. Are you asking me out to spite Michel?"

"No, Pierrette. Believe me ... I'm asking you out *despite* Michel."

"Honestly?"

"Honestly!"

"Then I'll give you my number."

"It's okay, I've looked it up already."

Manetti was jolted from his memory trance by Ann Stevenson's voice. "Rocco, are you all right?"

For a moment, he was disoriented. "Yes, of course! Don't I look all right?"

"Frankly, no. You're just sitting there, staring out the window."

"Just sitting here admiring the view. However, I'll go back to work if you insist."

CHAPTER SIX

AT SIX FIFTEEN on Wednesday evening, Manetti was ushered into the lounge of the University Club. Alastair Drake, ensconced in a leather wing chair, was waiting for him.

"No one can overhear us here," said Drake, as they shook hands. "What will you have?"

Manetti asked for Scotch, and Drake asked for *the usual*.

"What's *the usual*?" asked Manetti.

"Perrier! Apparently, the pills I'm taking are allergic to alcohol." Drake grimaced. "Enjoy your Scotch."

"I'll be consumed with guilt."

"Do you want to switch to Perrier then?"

"No, I'll stick with Scotch and guilt."

"Are you getting away for the long weekend?" asked Drake.

"Yes, Warren and I are flying up to the Mountain Lake camp tomorrow, and the plane can drop me off at Lake Muskoka on Friday afternoon. Then I'll sit on the dock and ponder the fate of Lunex. Are you going north?"

"No. Since Beth died, I've more or less surrendered the cottage to my two sons. The place will be wall-to-wall grandchildren, all screaming in unison."

"Why don't you spend the weekend with us? We don't have any screaming grandchildren yet, and Pierrette would be delighted to see you. She's been alone at the cottage for the last few weeks and would welcome some company."

"Thanks, but I don't want to interrupt your pondering. Since Noramet's the elephant in the room, let's shoot it now ... so we can enjoy dinner later. Why don't you start by giving me a blow-by-blow on your meeting with Graydon. I know what happened, but I'd like to get a feel for *who shoved whom*, and how hard."

Drake stared into his glass as Manetti related his interview with Graydon and Armstrong. Then he chuckled. "I'm glad you gave the middle finger to Fennell. You might as well go down in flames."

"Don't be a bastard, Alastair, you know why I'm here."

"Let me guess. You're looking for a white knight who'll rescue you from Noramet, and also take you to dinner."

"You're a good guesser."

"And you're a great optimist ... except for the dinner part."

"Come on, Alastair, you own 24 percent of us already. That's a great head start. My group will tender our shares to a Laurentian offer. There's another 30 percent. It'd be a slam dunk for Laurentian."

"Yes. In a Hollywood movie, we'd ride over the hill, rescue Lunex from the evil raider, and everyone would live happily ever after ... everyone except the villainous Fennell."

"What's wrong with that scenario?"

"Nothing, if this were cinema. Rocco, old friend, don't think *cinema*, think *prize fight*."

"That's exactly how I do think of it, as a prize fight for Mountain Lake—a fantastic prize."

"In the far corner, wearing black trunks and a pugilistic snarl, and snorting fire, is Noramet, North America's premier gold producer, a company which is cash-rich and hungry for a gold acquisition. In the near corner, wearing white trunks and an apologetic grin, and sipping Perrier, is Laurentian—"

"A mining giant, which is as big or bigger than Noramet," interrupted Manetti.

"A base-metals company, which made a strategic decision to abandon the gold business," countered Drake.

"As a result of which it owns 24 percent of the prize already," said Manetti, "a huge weight advantage in the match—"

"As a result of which we have 24 percent of the prize without having to raise a glove."

Manetti shook his head in frustration. "I'm offering you control of the biggest goldfield ever discovered in Canada—it's going to be vast—and you're telling me you'll settle for some cash, or a few shares of Noramet?"

"Quite a lot of cash, I imagine, and quite a few shares. Let's be candid, Rocco. I'm on your side. You know that. But all you're offering Laurentian is a bloody nose. All you're *offering* Laurentian is a slugfest with Noramet."

"No, if my group tenders to a Laurentian bid, and we will, I'm offering you control of Lunex, which means controlling the biggest goldfield ever discovered in Canada."

"Speaking for myself, I'm tempted, but how do I tempt my Board? Assuming Noramet offers a large takeover premium for Lunex, and it will, why wouldn't the Laurentian Board be well-advised to cash in our Lunex shares and skip off to the bank? We can certainly use the money."

"The Laurentian Board will look colossally stupid when the mining world in general, and Laurentian shareholders in particular, wake up to the fact that you sold 24 percent of a bonanza for a relative pittance. No matter what takeover premium Noramet offers Lunex shareholders, Fennell will be stealing Mountain Lake, because the full scope of the orebody isn't yet known and therefore can't have been fairly factored into our share price. Take my word for it, Alastair, Mountain Lake is going to make history."

"I concede that Mountain Lake is a bonanza," replied Drake, "so why wouldn't the Laurentian Board be well-advised to forgo the cash, tender our Lunex shares for Noramet shares, and let Noramet develop the bonanza. The only change would be a change in operators: Noramet personnel instead of your people. From the perspective of the Laurentian Board, what's wrong with that scenario? Convince me."

"I'd say the main thing wrong with that scenario *is* the change of operators. Apart from that, Laurentian would lose respect in the mining industry, not to mention self-respect, if you let the Yankee raiders snatch Mountain Lake from under your nose."

"I've been waiting for you to play the *patriotism* card, the last refuge of scoundrels."

"If only scoundrels want Canadians to develop Canada's natural resources, then I'm a proud scoundrel. We certainly can't look to our retarded politicians to protect Canada."

"Amen to that! However, we are where we are, so let's review the bidding. Having made a strategic decision to withdraw from the gold business, Laurentian sold its gold properties to Lunex. That's divestment step number one. Now it looks like we may have an opportunity to sell our Lunex shares at a fat takeover premium. That's divestment step number two. That gets us out of the gold business, and with our coffers full of cash. What could be sweeter? If the Laurentian directors believe that Mountain Lake is in fact a bonanza, and I expect I'll convince them of that, then we'll tender our Lunex shares for Noramet shares and forgo the cash."

"All that would be fine if Mountain Lake were just a run-of-the-mill goldfield, but it isn't. It's vast! Opportunity is knocking loudly at your door."

"I hear Rocco Manetti knocking. Is that the same thing?"

"I'm opportunity's messenger."

"Perhaps *opportunistic's* messenger."

Manetti shrugged. "This is your big chance, Alastair. Don't blow it."

"Big chance, maybe; big gamble, certainly. Here's another scenario for you: Noramet steps aside, lets Laurentian acquire Lunex, and then launches a takeover bid for Laurentian."

"Laurentian's bigger than Noramet. You could fight them off."

"Could we? They're cash rich and hungry, and at current market prices, Laurentian is undervalued. Noramet would be getting a bargain. In all honesty, Rocco, I don't think I could persuade my Board to launch a white-knight takeover bid for Lunex. We're supposed to be concentrating on our core businesses, and gold isn't one of our core businesses."

"With respect, gold should become one of your core businesses. If Lunex had the chance to pick up a windfall like Mountain Lake, we'd jump at it."

"When I was young and inexperienced, I'd sometimes spring for windfalls. Now I'm too wary and wily and weary to spring for windfalls. However, I'll spring for dinner, so let's go upstairs."

CHAPTER SEVEN

AS MANETTI AND Drake were settling in at the University Club, Macdonald was ambling along the underground concourse from First Canadian Place to the Toronto Dominion Centre, a route he seldom took. He usually left his office around six-thirty or seven and went straight down to the First Canadian Place parking garage to meet his driver. Tonight, he was caught up in a river of office workers funnelling down the concourse to catch subway and commuter trains. Tonight, he was mingling with the hoi polloi.

Although the rest of the world was in a rush and rushing, Macdonald was in no hurry and made no effort to go with the flow, and since he was much too large to be swept aside, the river was forced to flow around this rock in the rapids. At the Wellington Street exit, he took the stairs to street level and completed his stroll to the Toronto Club, where he was ushered into a private dining room. Bill Graydon and Jill Armstrong were waiting for him, well-rehearsed and waiting.

After introductions and some Graydonesque name-dropping, they got down to business. "We appreciate your coming over on such short notice, Ross. I know you're wondering what this is all about, and I want to explain. However, I'm authorized to do so on the express understanding that you'll keep these discussions in strict confidence. Is that okay with you?"

"No problem, unless you're about to confess to a murder."

"Nothing like that," said Graydon, pretending to be amused. "We represent Noramet Inc., which wants to acquire the Mountain Lake properties owned by Lunex." He paused for a reaction, but Macdonald didn't react. "Jill and I approached Dr. Manetti on Tuesday, but I'm afraid our approach wasn't well received. It would be more accurate to say it was bluntly rejected."

"Manetti's a blunt fellow," replied Macdonald. "There are better words to describe him, but I'll not use them with Ms. Armstrong present."

"We'll leave it at *blunt*," said Graydon. There was a pause, while drinks were ordered, after which Graydon continued. "Although Dr. Manetti's reaction was anticipated, approaching him was a necessary first step. So, now Noramet is gearing up for a takeover bid, which of course, brings Laurentian into the picture. If you don't want to go any further with this discussion, tell me now."

"Keep going."

"Good! Well, it's obviously not going to be a friendly bid, and we assume that the Lunex gang would support a Laurentian counter-bid, so it would be prudent for Noramet to discover how Laurentian might respond to a Noramet bid."

"I can't tell you how Laurentian would respond," said Macdonald, "but I can tell you how Ross Macdonald would respond. I'd pray for one or more competing bidders, the more the merrier, following which Laurentian would tender our Lunex stock to the highest bidder."

"That's the sensible course," said Graydon. "Noramet can and will outbid any competitors, with the possible exception of Laurentian, which has a 24 percent head start. What we'd like to know is whether Laurentian might become a white knight for Lunex."

"And you want me to turn informant."

"I wouldn't characterize it like that," said Graydon. "Would you, Jill?"

"No, not at all," replied Armstrong. "We're not trying to influence Laurentian's decision one way or the other. We simply want to know whether Laurentian would support or oppose a Noramet bid."

"In my opinion, we'd be daft to become a white knight. However, it won't be my decision."

"Not yours alone," said Graydon, "but you're on the Laurentian Board, and you're the president of the company, so presumably it's fair to say that you're one of the directing minds over there."

Macdonald nodded.

"And presumably, you'll know how things are shaping up," continued Graydon.

Macdonald nodded again. "That's true enough. However, that decision may not be made until Noramet launches its bid, in which case, it'll be too late for a heads up."

"We recognize that. However, in light of Dr. Manetti's reaction, I'll wager he'll soon be knocking on Laurentian's door for protection. In fact, he may have been knocking on your door already. That was part of our strategy in making the direct approach to him, to smoke him out of his cave and drive him into the open."

Dinner was served, and the conversation turned to city politics for a few minutes; then Graydon steered it back to Lunex. "As I said, I wouldn't be at all surprised if Dr. Manetti had been knocking on your door already."

"If he has, he's been knocking on Drake's door." Macdonald beamed a disingenuous grin. "Why don't you ask Drake?"

"I'm sure you know the answer to that one," said Graydon with a tight smile. "Among other reasons, we understand he's a personal friend of Dr. Manetti, and as such, might be expected to take an unsympathetic view of our bid."

"Yes, Drake thinks the sun rises and sets on Manetti. I know well enough why you're approaching me instead of Drake, I just wanted to hear you say it. And now that you've said it, I don't feel any less of a mole."

"Look, Ross, I expected your initial reaction would be negative. I expected you to have reservations; that's to your credit. However, I'd really appreciate your talking it over with Dick Fennell. He better than I can explain Noramet's position, and he better than I can assure you that we're not trying to suborn Ross Macdonald."

"I hear you, but the acid test for me is whether I'd be embarrassed to read in the *Report on Business* that I'd been having secret discussions with Noramet."

"So would we, my friend. So would we. That's why you'd never read it in the *Report on Business* or anywhere else, and that's why we're having this and any future discussions in strict privacy and confidence. That said, we wouldn't consider asking you to do anything illegal. Look, if you still have reservations after talking to Dick Fennell, then that'll be an end of it. We won't try to pressure you. You have my word on that. Talk it over with Dick, strictly off the record on both sides. That's all I'm asking. It was Dick who asked me to get in touch with you; I assume from what he said that you know each other."

"I've met him on a couple of occasions."

"He thinks very highly of you. Dick said that he'd be happy to come up to Toronto, but he thinks a meeting in New York would be more anonymous. You mentioned on the phone that you'd be in New York tomorrow. Any chances you could schedule an hour for Noramet?"

"Not during the day, but I guess I could stay over."

"We'd really appreciate that, Ross." Graydon clapped Macdonald on the shoulder. "How about dinner at the Commerce Club, say six thirty. Does that work for you?"

"I guess so. Frankly, I'm still feeling a bit uneasy, but I guess there's nothing wrong with having dinner with you guys."

"Nothing wrong at all. Believe me, Ross, we're not trying to recruit a mole," said Graydon. "We want to make sure you understand where we're coming from. That's all. I think you owe it to Laurentian, and to yourself, to at least hear us out."

Graydon walked Macdonald as far as the room door, clapped him on the shoulder again, and shook his hand warmly. "If you fly up on Friday morning, you can still get a jump on the Friday afternoon exodus. That's what I plan to do. Canadian summers are short, and we can ill-afford to miss the Labour Day weekend."

Graydon returned to the table and poured himself another coffee. "How do you think that went?"

"He's nibbling at the bait," replied Armstrong, "but he's nervous."

"He's nervous all right. Even I was having trouble suborning him and disclaiming subornation at one and the same time."

"You're too modest. Does Dick Fennell really 'think very highly' of Macdonald?"

"Not that I've heard," Graydon smirked. "Remind me to remind Dick that he does."

"You're evil! Why didn't you mention Option C?"

"We'll raise Option C tomorrow night, by which time he'll have figured it out for himself and think he's smarter than we are. Now, tell me what your famous feminine instincts tell you about our friend Macdonald."

"The bad news is that he's shrewd and nervous. However, I think you can land the fish, if you're careful."

"What's the good news?"

"Four things! One, he smells cash and will support the Noramet bid. Two, he dislikes Manetti and has good reason to fear him. Three, whether or not he dislikes Drake personally, they're obviously not hand-in-glove. Four, he's a common bloke with pretensions, so Dick Fennell's Ivy League patter should impress him. All in all, he's predisposed to be our mole, if you can convince him that black is white."

"Any other vulnerabilities?"

"Yes, *vanity.* He's vain, like most males, and can be flattered. Also, he's a horny bastard."

"*Horny!* What makes you say that?"

"He spent a lot of time surreptitiously ogling my breasts."

"They're very shapely breasts."

"Whatever they are, they're useful for smoking out horny bastards. Anyway, I think sex is an Achilles heel for Ross Macdonald."

"Just because he was checking you out doesn't make him a horny bastard."

"I think it does. Have Noramet send a girl to his room tomorrow night. I'll bet you a hundred bucks he won't send her away."

"You've been reading too many spy novels. Neither Noramet nor Thorne Sullivan would sink to such immoral tactics."

"In that case, I'll do my best to quell the nasty rumours."

"You're too cynical by half. Even if we did adopt your scandalous suggestion, just how would you prove your bet?"

"I thought you guys all publish your score cards."

CHAPTER
EIGHT

AT DRAKE'S REQUEST the maitre d' escorted Manetti and him to a "quiet table." After their orders were taken, Manetti resumed his pitch. "At the risk of causing you indignation, I don't expect to see another Mountain Lake in my lifetime, and you're our only hope, Alastair. If Laurentian won't fight for Lunex, then Noramet will get us for sure."

"Rocco, why don't you just hold your nose and put Mountain Lake on the auction block? That's all Fennell wants. Noramet would go away and leave Lunex alone. Last week, you blackmailed me and the other Lunex Directors by threatening that you and your team would quit *en bloc* if we tried to shop Mountain Lake—"

"Not blackmail, just timely advice."

"You've got us Lunex Directors over a barrel, and you know it. If we deal Mountain Lake to Noramet, your group will quit *en blo*c, but your group *is* Lunex. I call that blackmail."

"I call that 'timely advice'."

"There's something you're not telling me, Rocco. What's the missing piece?"

"There is a missing piece," replied Manetti, "and I guess you're entitled to know: I'm an alumnus of Noramet."

"Yes, I know you had a stint there. So what?"

"I was there for a little over three years, back in the early eighties."

"And you're still smarting because they had the good sense to fire you."

"No, I quit. I wish they'd never hired me. I've discovered some great orebodies in my career, but I've only discovered two bonanzas: Pericatu in Chile and now Mountain Lake."

"You discovered Pericatu?" Drake raised his eyebrows. "Good for you! I didn't know that."

"There's no way you could have known, because it was never acknowledged. There are still a few people around Noramet who know the story, Fennell and Doyle for two. I had a good exploration team, but the geology was mine. At the time of the discovery, my team and I were abruptly *re-assigned* and then, presto, the credit went to the then Vice President of Exploration, a suit who never discovered an orebody in his life, not before, and not after. A suit who never left Head Office except to go home at five o'clock."

"You had a rough introduction to corporate politics. I don't blame you for being bitter."

"I was bitter at first, but then I realized they'd done me a big favour by showing me the true Noramet colours. I was an idealistic young explorationist, and naïve."

"I'm afraid infighting and back-stabbing are chronic diseases of corporate life."

"I'm afraid you're right. Anyway, I was ready, willing, and able to walk away from Noramet infighting and back-stabbing ... so I walked. I got quit of the bastards before they got the golden handcuffs on me. Now, more than a quarter century later, Lunex discovers Mountain Lake, and surprise, surprise, Noramet's trying to shoulder me out again. That's the missing piece of your puzzle."

"I understand." Drake paused for a long moment. "Rocco, it's my turn to cause you indigestion. Let's suppose I were reckless enough to recommend the white-knight option to my Board, and let's suppose my Board were reckless enough to accept my recommendation. If I did all that for Lunex, I'd expect a significant quid pro quo from you."

"Now you're talking. It goes without saying that we'd pay a hefty break fee in the event Noramet outbids you."

"Yes, if we went to war with Noramet and lost, we'd certainly want a big break fee, but that's not the quid pro quo I'm talking about. If Laurentian were to win and acquire Lunex, I'd want you to succeed me as Chairman and CEO of Laurentian."

"No way, Alastair! Look, I'm honoured, but it's an honour I don't want. I don't want to be a captain of industry."

"You already are. You like to pretend you're not. Anyway, I never thought you did want the job or would want the job."

"I'm glad you understand. I wouldn't know how to run a big corporation like Laurentian, even if I did want—"

"Say no more," interrupted Drake. "I understand your position, now you must understand mine. My offer's a take-it-or-leave-it offer. I'm not going to promote the white-knight option to my Board unless you agree to succeed me."

"That's recruitment by coercion."

"I'd call it 'timely advice.' In my experience, the best CEOs never chase the top job; they accept it graciously when asked to do so. You certainly fit that profile, except for the *gracious acceptance* part. I neither wanted nor needed this job, but I got used to it ... and I've been reasonably good at it. You'd get used to it too, and you'd do even better at it than I."

"I don't have the qualifications."

"You're infinitely better qualified than I was. Look at my background. I grew up in Devon, the son of an English clergyman, and read history at Oxford. I should have ended up as a history professor at some obscure red-brick university. Instead, I ended up as CEO of Laurentian."

"You're a marketing genius; that's why you're running Laurentian. What do I know about running a big multinational? I'm just a simple geologist—"

"I've heard that song before. You're also an excellent manager, who knows the mining industry inside and out. Look at it this way: If Lunex became a subsidiary of Laurentian, and if you became the CEO of Laurentian, you'd be *numero uno* in the whole organization, which means you'd be at liberty to fondle good-looking drill cores from time to time—always within the bounds of geological decency, of course. You could even run into the wilderness occasionally and look for gold, but not often and not for long. Warren could run Lunex; he's ready. A few minutes ago, you said I didn't hear opportunity knocking. Let me return the challenge."

"I thought Ross Macdonald was your designated successor."

"Ross thinks so too."

"So, may I ask what happened there?"

"In the context of this discussion, you're entitled to ask. *Entre nous*—and strictly *entre nous*—Ross has been chasing the top job, coveting the top job, salivating for the top job... cardinal sins in my view. Quite apart from that, a CEO must lead, not bully. Ross gets results, but he earns no respect or loyalty. Whether or not you accept my coercive offer, I'll be blackballing Ross as my successor."

"Then why haven't you ditched him before now?"

"Everything in good time. When he doesn't succeed me, he'll resign. Ross is a self-correcting problem."

"So, you want to retire, you want quit of Macdonald, and you're targeting me as a quick and convenient substitute."

"I'd call you a *pain-in-the-ass* substitute," replied Drake. "You're a damsel-in-distress who comes to a peace-loving white knight and begs him to enter the lists against a warlike black knight who's been hitting on her. '*The odds are stacked against me*,' says the retirement-minded white knight, '*but if I beat the odds and rescue you from the black knight, I want to retire and I want you to succeed me.*' 'Oh, I *couldn't do that,'* says the damsel-in-distress. *'I don't think I'd like your job'.*"

"Damsels-in-distress don't morph into white knights."

"I have a granddaughter who'd be happy to debate that point, and she'd win. Anyway, I'm not going to approach my Board unless and until you agree to succeed me, so please yourself."

"I don't have any choice then. You have all the cards."

"You're gracious to a fault."

"Okay, I accept. If and when Laurentian takes Lunex into protective custody, I'll be pleased and honoured to succeed you as Chairman and CEO of Laurentian. Is that better?"

"Much better, but it lacks the ring of sincerity."

"Do you have unfettered authority to designate your own successor? I mean, maybe the Laurentian Board won't share your enthusiasm for me, and your lack of enthusiasm for Macdonald."

"I've already discussed you as a potential candidate with several of our key directors, and as a straight recruitment, you'd be welcomed with open arms. No problem there! I haven't floated the idea of Laurentian acquiring Lunex, much less the highly problematic prospect of Laurentian having to go to war with Noramet in order to acquire Lunex."

"If you beat the odds, and if I have to step into your shoes, would I also have to move into that over-sized office of yours?"

"Yes, it goes with the job, and you'd also have to start dressing like a grown-up."

"I never thought I'd end up as a suit."

"*In* a suit, not *as* a suit. There's a difference, Rocco. You can be stuffed into a dress shirt without being a stuffed shirt. Do you think of me as a suit?"

"No, Alastair, I don't. Nor do I think of you as a stuffed shirt."

"Glad to hear it. You should never insult a prospective white knight."

"If I ever have to move into that over-sized office of yours, would you be insulted if I took a lawn mower to the broadloom?"

"Cut anything you like, except dividends and pensions. However, Rocco, I greatly fear that you won't be moving into my office, because I gravely doubt that Laurentian will be acquiring Lunex. I hope I'm wrong. I'll do everything in my power to prove myself wrong."

CHAPTER
NINE

AT SIX O'CLOCK on Thursday evening, Richard Fennell and Bill Graydon were in a private dining room at the Commerce Club, lounging in wing chairs and drinking martinis, waiting for their prey to arrive.

Contrary to appearances, both Fennell and Graydon were hard at work. Jill Armstrong had prepared a background report on Macdonald, including notes on their Toronto Club meeting, and Fennell was studying that report closely. For his part, Graydon was trying to anticipate Fennell's questions, and trying to envision how the upcoming interview with Macdonald would play out.

"Good briefing document," said Fennell, returning the report to Graydon. "Your Jill Armstrong is smart—and damn good looking, if she's the girl I'm thinking of. You should bring her along next time. Better still, send her down to see me some time. It's high time for her to become better acquainted with Noramet, and *vice versa.*" Fennell surrendered to sexual fantasy for a moment and then continued. "Anyway, if Macdonald is as unpopular at Laurentian as she says he is, that's very good news for us. I wonder how she uncovered his *Black Angus* nickname and all that other personal stuff?"

"Thorne Sullivan thoroughness."

"A woman's thoroughness. It takes a woman to get that kind of detail. When Macdonald arrives, I'll spin it as though you haven't had much of a chance to brief me on yesterday's meeting. That'll give me an open field." He leaned across and slapped Graydon on the knee. "Cheer up, Bill! I know my lines. I'm to make Macdonald believe 'I think highly of him' and I'm to feed him that guff about keeping Manetti in place at Lunex. I fear I'll grow a Pinnochio nose because I certainly don't think highly of Macdonald. He's a bloody traitor. And I fully intend to sack that cocky bastard Manetti at the first opportunity, along with the rest of his crew. *David and Goliath*, my ass! I'm going to mop the floor with Manetti, Ransom, and the rest of them. All of them. It's only six twenty, so we've got time for another drink before Judas arrives."

At that moment, Judas was trapped in a taxi, which in turn was trapped in a slow-moving traffic jam. It was a few minutes shy of seven o'clock when the cab pulled up to the Commerce Club, and the mantle clock began chiming the hour as Macdonald was ushered into the Alexander Hamilton Room.

"My apologies, gentlemen." Macdonald looked flustered. "Believe it or not, I left the Plaza Hotel at just past six."

"We believe you," said Fennell, stepping forward and shaking hands. "We should be apologizing to you for the 24/7 traffic jams in Manhattan, and for the heat wave."

"Yes, it's stinking hot out there, although I guess I can't blame you guys for the traffic or the temperature. At least the cab was air-conditioned."

Graydon and Macdonald shook hands. "Thanks for staying over, Ross."

"You need a drink," said Fennell, "and Bill and I are ready for refills."

Noting their high colour, Macdonald guessed that this wouldn't be their first refill. "I'll have the same," he said, gesturing towards the empty martini glasses. Then he paused for a moment to take in his surroundings.

Apart from the cluster of large leather chairs—clustered to no good purpose around a dead fireplace—the room was furnished with a large mahogany dining table and a large mahogany buffet. The stately table, designed for a stately twelve, was set for a lonely three.

Heavy drapes shut off the windows and shut out the steaming city, although an occasional siren, muffled and distant, managed to penetrate the hushed and air-conditioned world of the Commerce Club. A dozen or more illuminated oil paintings hung on the burnished oak panelling. Macdonald was correct in guessing that they were significant canvases, and he promised himself a tour of the gallery at some stage during the evening.

"In Scotland, we'd call this a *braw* room," observed Macdonald as he sat down.

Fennell and Graydon took chairs on either side of their target. "*Braw*," echoed Fennell. "That's a good word for it. My favourite room in this club. I always reserve it, even when the party's too small for the space."

"It reminds me of Boodles in London," said Macdonald.

"*Boodles*," repeated Fennell. "On St. James, just down from Piccadilly."

"That's right."

"I've been invited to many London clubs in my day but never to Boodles. Are you a member there?"

"Me? No! I'm a poor boy from Glasgow with a few well-connected friends."

"The President of Laurentian Mining can hardly claim to be a *poor boy*," said Graydon.

"I *was* a poor boy," replied Macdonald. "Anyway, it takes more than money to get into Boodles; it's not like North American clubs."

Fennell frowned at the slighting comment but let it pass. "Why don't we get the business out of the way before dinner? They serve a decent meal at this North American club, and there are better things to talk about than gold properties. Right, Bill?"

"My sentiments exactly," said Graydon, picking up his cue. "I'd much rather talk about London clubs."

"Graydon's in love with England, like the Canadian colonial he is," said Fennell. "I think he still expects the U.S.A. to pay war reparations for the Boston Tea Party. Well, to business then. Bill and I had to go over a few other matters before you arrived, so I'm afraid I haven't heard much about yesterday's meeting at the Toronto Club. I'll lead off, but let me apologize in advance if I cover some of the same ground."

The drinks arrived and Fennell fell silent until the waiter left. "I presume Bill told you that Noramet intends to acquire the Mountain Lake properties owned by Lunex."

Macdonald nodded.

"Until a couple of days ago, we had three options, now there are only two. Option A was to acquire the Mountain Lake properties by an outright purchase. However, Option A is a non-starter; I assume Bill told you what happened there."

"Yes, I understand Manetti turned you down flat."

"That was no surprise to Bill or to me, but we had to approach him. That leaves Noramet with Options B and C."

Macdonald leaned forward, propping his elbows on his knees. "Let's make sure I have the algebra straight. Option B would be a hostile takeover bid for Lunex, and Option C would be a hostile takeover bid for Laurentian."

"Precisely," replied Fennell. "Thorne Sullivan thinks and speaks algebraically, and I've fallen into their ways. Did you and Bill discuss all this yesterday?"

"We discussed your Option B," replied Macdonald.

"Then I congratulate you on deducing Option C without benefit of investment bankers. As you know, a Noramet takeover bid for Lunex is problematic, because Laurentian could block us by launching a counter-bid supported by the Manetti gang. If that were to happen, we'd have to retreat with our tail between our legs, which neither Noramet nor I ever do, or else we'd have to outbid Laurentian by increasing our offer into the stratosphere, which would be bad business, or else we'd have to pursue Option C. However, having made a run at Lunex in the first instance, our ability to switch gears and go after Laurentian instead of Lunex would be impaired. Is that a fair statement, Bill?"

"Yes, the optics would be terrible," agreed Graydon. "Thorne Sullivan will advise Noramet to make a bid for Lunex only if and only when we have a high degree of confidence that Laurentian won't try to block the bid. Absent that, we'll recommend that Noramet bypass Lunex altogether and make a bid for Laurentian in the first instance."

"There it is in a nutshell, Ross. However, since we're only interested in Mountain Lake, Option C seems Draconian, to say the least. On the other hand, there's a strong business case to be made in support of that Draconian takeover. Right Bill?"

"Absolutely!" replied Graydon. "Diversification into base metals makes good business sense; and acquiring Laurentian makes good business sense. Thorne Sullivan is of the view that Laurentian is ripe for the picking."

Fennell shrugged. "There you have it, Ross. Mountain Lake may trigger a major diversification at Noramet. God moves in strange ways."

"Any advice for us?" asked Graydon.

"I don't know how to advise you," replied Macdonald, "and even if I did, I shouldn't be advising you. In fact, I'm not sure I should be here at all. However, since I am here, I don't mind repeating where I stand, and why ... as long as we're strictly off the record."

"Absolutely off the record," replied Fennell, "and please don't say anything that makes you feel compromised in the slightest."

"I won't, but I don't mind giving you the gospel according to Saint Macdonald: the same thing I told Bill and Ms. Armstrong yesterday, and the same thing I told Alastair Drake yesterday for that matter. Having made a deliberate decision to get out of the gold business, Laurentian should stay the hell out of the gold business. We're the largest shareholder of Lunex because they paid us in shares for our gold properties. At the time we'd have preferred cash. At least, I would have. On the other hand, Drake was always against abandoning the gold business, and has always taken a keen interest in Lunex. As you know, he's on the Lunex Board, and he's an enthusiastic and active Director over there. I think he regards Lunex as a Laurentian subsidiary." Macdonald shrugged dismissively. "As far as I'm concerned, our Lunex shares are nothing more nor less than a portfolio investment, whether Drake likes it or not. If Mountain Lake sparks a takeover bid for Lunex, and it looks like it has, or *better still*, competing takeover bids, which it yet might, then Laurentian should complete its original divestment program by selling to the highest bidder. Conversely, I would *and will* actively oppose any move by Laurentian to block a takeover bid for Lunex. End of sermon. Now if my name was Alastair Drake, you could rest easy."

"Do you think Alastair Drake will be minded to block our bid?" asked Graydon.

"I can't give you any assurance he won't. He's a great admirer of Manetti, which is why we sold our gold properties to Lunex in the first place. There's no doubt in my mind that Drake will at least give serious consideration to the idea of a counter-bid."

"Drake's far from stupid," said Fennell. "He'll surely recognize that we have Option C in our back pocket."

"I'll make good and sure he does," replied Macdonald. "I don't think I've been of much assistance to you."

"Knowing where you stand is of great assistance, Ross," replied Fennell, "and we want to reciprocate by letting you know where we stand. As we see it, Noramet will get Mountain Lake, by hook or by crook, sooner or later. We always get what we want, one way or another, sooner or later. However, a bid for Laurentian is clumsy, since all we really want is Mountain Lake. And, if you'll forgive a personal observation, I know of no reason why you should sacrifice your own career on Alastair Drake's altar. If you're slated to succeed Drake, as it appears to the outside world you are, your succession isn't far off. However, a Noramet takeover of Laurentian would almost certainly block your succession to that top job. I'm sorry to tell you that, but I think we should get all our cards on the table."

"Can you explain that last card?" asked Macdonald.

"I can and I will," said Fennell, "but since we have a good dinner in the offing, I won't beat around the bush. I'll talk to you the way I'd talk to my own brother."

"Be as blunt as you like," said Macdonald.

"Bluntly then, let's look at Options B and C as they impact Ross Macdonald, who—if I may say so as an outsider—has been doing a great job as President of Laurentian and richly deserves to succeed Alastair Drake as Chairman and CEO."

"I'm not sure Drake would say '*amen*' to that," said Macdonald.

"I'm sure he would," said Fennell. "However, whether he would or wouldn't, Option C is bad news for Ross Macdonald. If Noramet were forced to go after Laurentian instead of Lunex, we'd end up with a major nickel company on our hands. For my part, I'd be elated to have you take the helm at Laurentian, and I'd recommend you for the top job, but I'm afraid my Board would insist on parachuting a Noramet executive into the top job. That's how Noramet works. That's how Noramet has always done things. The Board might ask you to stay on as number two, but you'd be an outsider *vis a vis* our organization, and my Directors wouldn't let an outsider run the show. It's as simple as that. Let's look at Option B, the *win/win* scenario, in which Noramet launches a successful takeover bid for Lunex. In that event, Noramet intends to keep Manetti in place by keeping Lunex as a separate and distinct entity, and by giving him *carte blanche* to develop Mountain Lake. That will keep Manetti out of the Laurentian sphere and *ipso facto* eliminate him as a contender for the top job at Laurentian. He's a geologist's geologist and will jump at the chance to develop Mountain Lake, particularly when we make that a condition precedent to keeping his team employed and in place. He'll do it for the challenge, he'll do it for the money, and of greatest importance to him, he'll do it to protect the careers of his colleagues. I'm given to understand that he's excessively loyal to his Lunex colleagues—a commendable weakness, but a weakness nonetheless. Under the win/win scenario, Manetti stays on the job at Lunex, exactly where we want him, which should ensure your succession at Laurentian. Whether or not I'm right, that's how the universe looks to this outsider." Fennell signalled the waiter who was hovering discreetly out of earshot. "That's enough business for tonight, gentlemen. I'm getting hungry."

True to his word, Fennell didn't discuss business during dinner. Afterwards, his driver was waiting at the curb to deliver everyone home, first Graydon to the Waldorf Astoria, then Macdonald to the Plaza, and lastly Fennell to Noramet's Park Avenue apartment. As the car drew up to the Plaza, Fennell and Macdonald shook hands.

"It's been a pleasure meeting you again, Ross ... a great pleasure indeed. However this thing plays out, I know you'll keep our conversation in confidence."

"Absolutely! And *vice versa!*"

"Absolutely! I know you'll always act in the best interests of Laurentian and its shareholders, and at the risk of sounding presumptuous, I share your view that a Noramet takeover of Lunex is in the best interests of Laurentian and its shareholders. So, if there's anything you can do to move things in that direction, that would be great. If you can let Bill know which way the wind's blowing at Laurentian, that would be great too."

"I'll do what I can."

"I know you will, Ross, and I appreciate it."

"The decision may be made at next Wednesday's Board meeting," said Macdonald. "At least, Lunex is the sole agenda item for that meeting."

"Well, as you say, do what you can. Noramet appreciates its friends."

Macdonald looked uneasy. "Several planets appear to be in alignment, but anything I do will be for Laurentian, not for Noramet and not for Ross Macdonald."

"Of course, it will, Ross! Of course, it will! I'd be astonished and disappointed if you acted out of self-interest."

Macdonald went up to his room and telephoned for a five thirty wake-up call, grimacing as he contemplated tomorrow morning's rush to LaGuardia and the red-eye flight to Toronto. He threw his suit jacket on the bed, kicked off his shoes, loosened his tie, and poured himself a nightcap. He had a lot to mull over before he could sleep.

As he gazed down absently on Central Park South, his mind was churning through the realities facing Laurentian, and more importantly, Ross Macdonald. He was lost in thought and didn't hear the shy tap. He did hear the second tap and strode impatiently to the door, irritated that he was being interrupted by a room check. The young woman in the hallway was definitely not a chambermaid.

"Mr. Macdonald?"

"Nancy? What are you doing here?"

"I'm Tracy. Were you expecting Nancy?" She slipped deftly into the room, leaving him holding an open door to no good purpose.

"I wasn't expecting anybody." Macdonald let the door swing shut. "I mistook you for one of my daughter's friends. Who are you?"

She put an arm around his waist. "I'm Nancy or Tracy or whoever you want me to be." Then she read his astonished expression. "You really weren't expecting anyone, were you?"

"That's what I said."

"I'm so sorry, there's been a mix-up." She moved towards the door.

He took her arm gently. "Not so fast! I said I *wasn't* expecting anybody. However, you may be a welcome surprise."

She turned back with a demure smile. "I hope so, Ross."

"Will you have a drink then?" He gestured towards the bottle of Macallan.

"I'd love a glass of white wine."

"White wine it is. I'll call room service."

She pointed to a cabinet. "What's in there?"

"Of course! of course! The bar fridge. You must have been here before."

"Maybe." She settled into a large easy chair and glanced around. "It's a pretty room, don't you think?"

"I hadn't thought about it."

He uncorked a bottle and delivered a glass of wine to her. "I hope this is okay. Anyway, it's what the Plaza has on offer."

She sipped the wine and nodded. "It's a very nice California chardonnay. More than okay."

Macdonald looked across the room at the bottle but couldn't read the label. "Can you read the label from here?"

"No, but I can taste it from here."

"A connoisseur," he said, retrieving his tumbler of Scotch and looking ill-at-ease. "Cheers then!"

Macdonald had tangled with prostitutes on a few occasions, but they had all been hookers who dressed like hookers and acted like hookers. He couldn't believe this well-groomed, discreetly-dressed young woman was a whore. "You're a dead ringer for Nancy, my daughter's roommate at U of T."

"U of T?"

"University of Toronto," he replied absently. He was trying to remember Nancy's last name. It troubled him to think that Nancy, and his own daughter for that matter, were old enough for the sex trade. They were still just kids. This girl was just a kid too.

She was somebody's daughter. "Where did you get my name and room number?"

"From the agency. I guess someone wanted to surprise you."

"Well, they've succeeded. Do you know what you're doing?"

"Satisfaction guaranteed!"

"I didn't mean that. You're just a kid. Why are you in this business?"

"For fun and profit, Ross. I'm not a white slave, if that's what's worrying you … and I'm old enough to vote, if *that's* what's worrying you."

Macdonald shrugged and produced his wallet. It was Tracy's turn to be embarrassed. "Ross, please, that's all been taken care of."

"By whom?"

"I get my assignments from the agency, and I don't ask questions. If I had to guess, I'd say you have a well-heeled and anonymous friend who thinks you might be lonely tonight."

"Or thinks he can set me up?"

"What are you worried about, Ross? Private detectives in the hallway? Miniature cameras in my bra? Body mikes? That kind of thing?"

"It's been known to happen."

She crossed the room and stretched out on the bed. "You're much too suspicious. As far as detectives in the hallway go, take a look and then put on the burglar chain. As far as hidden cameras and body mikes go, why don't you search me?"

Macdonald suddenly slapped his forehead, a gesture of frustration and embarrassment. "I'll have to phone room service for a condom."

She shook her head dismissively. "I doubt condoms are on the menu. I thought the Boy Scout motto was *Be Prepared.*"

He caught a guilty glimpse of thigh as she clambered off the bed and made for the door. With sinking heart and rising erection, he realized that she was about to leave. "I could call a bell boy," he proposed lamely, trying to snatch victory from the jaws of defeat.

She didn't reply but suddenly turned back, producing a foil packet from her purse, along with a flourish and a broad *gotcha* grin. "The Girl Scout motto is *Better French Safe than Sorry,*" she said. "Now, where were we?"

He returned the grin, somewhat shamefacedly. "I was going to search you for hidden mikes."

"I like that idea," she replied, and climbed back on the bed.

It was a good half hour before they resumed their conversation—a very good half hour.

"You look just like Nancy," said Macdonald, as if to himself.

"You've seen Nancy in the buff?"

"You look like her from the shoulders up. Tell me, what do you do other times?"

"You mean when I'm not *escorting?*" She smiled. "By day, I'm a graduate student at New York University."

"Bullshit you are."

"Bullshit I am." She shrugged, indicating that she wouldn't try to convince him.

"Are you really?"

"Really I am."

"You don't look any older than my daughter."

"What's she studying?"

"I'm not exactly sure; English or History or something. What are you studying?"

"Psychology. I'm in a pre-doctoral program. You might call this fieldwork."

Macdonald stroked her hair as he absorbed that information. "I guess this is the first time I've made love to a shrink."

"Life's full of new adventures, Ross. This is the first time I've had sex with a Scot."

CHAPTER
TEN

AS HE RESPONDED to the five thirty wake up call, Macdonald was bitterly regretting his travel instructions. If only his secretary had used her head, she'd have ignored those instructions and booked him on a later flight. He reminded himself that he needed a new secretary, someone who wouldn't slavishly follow instructions, someone with initiative and imagination.

During the ride to LaGuardia, he settled back in the limousine, closed his eyes, and relived his encounter with Tracy. Not until the plane took off did he reluctantly say goodbye to her and turn to business—an exercise of willpower, which was impeded by frequent and prolix announcements, first in English and then in French.

He flagged down an Air Canada attendant as she passed. "No wonder Americans fly *American*. Any way you can turn her off?" Her only response was a professional smile—the tolerant and distant smile she'd been trained to bestow on cranky business-class passengers. However, his complaint coincided with the head girl's finale, which prompted the flight attendant to look back and beam a conspiratorial smile at Macdonald, coupled with a surreptitious *V for victory* salute.

Better than the middle finger, he thought, returning the salute. Macdonald refocused his mind and became immediately absorbed in the looming challenges. His first challenge was to discover Drake's intentions, so that he could give Noramet a timely heads-up. His second challenge would be to dissuade Drake from trying to block Noramet's bid, if in fact Drake was so inclined. His third challenge would be to derail Drake's recommendation to the Board, if Drake intended to promote the white-knight option. Those were daunting challenges, particularly since there were real tensions between Drake and him. Their personalities had always clashed, so much so that he'd often wondered why Drake hadn't blocked his promotion to the number-two job. He freely admitted to himself that, in reverse circumstances, he certainly would have blackballed Drake.

Macdonald had to concede, reluctantly, that Laurentian had flourished under the ever-popular Drake, but he firmly believed the company's success was due in equal measure to himself: the hard-nosed and kickass President and Chief Operating Officer. He had always regarded Drake's management style as weak, shot through with unnecessary concern for the well-being of Laurentian employees. He wondered whether the Laurentian Board had also recognized that Drake was weak and needed a tough chief operating officer to give the organization some backbone. Perhaps Drake *had* tried to blackball him, and perhaps the Board had overruled Drake. He'd never know.

Macdonald reminded himself that a leopard can't change its spots, even if it wants to, and he further reminded himself that this particular leopard didn't want to. When he became the alpha leopard, the mentoring would stop and the law of the jungle would start.

He mused on the possibility—the remote possibility—that Drake would come to his senses and recommend that Laurentian tender its Lunex shares to a Noramet bid. If so, Macdonald could pass on the good news to Noramet and everybody would live happily ever after. That was the easy but more improbable scenario.

The tough and probable scenario was that Drake would recommend to the Board that Laurentian play the white knight by making a counter-offer for Lunex. If that were to happen, the Laurentian

Directors might well support Drake, since they regarded him as half business genius and half saint. Macdonald would have to do some pre-emptive manoeuvring behind-the-scenes—some clever and covert lobbying—to influence a few key Directors in favour of Noramet's bid.

Macdonald didn't doubt for a moment that, if Laurentian got in Noramet's way, Fennell could and would switch targets and make a takeover bid for Laurentian instead of Lunex. If Drake got Board approval to roll the dice, he'd be gambling with Macdonald's career, not his own. Drake had nothing to lose. Macdonald had everything to lose.

Since there was little likelihood of Drake sharing confidences with him, he'd have to ferret out Drake's intentions by stealth, and he'd have to do it quickly.

By the time the plane was cruising high above Niagara Falls, Macdonald had convinced himself that he had a god-sent mission to save Laurentian by thwarting Drake, and by the time the plane landed at Pearson International, he'd settled on an action plan. Muskoka would have to wait until tomorrow.

CHAPTER
ELEVEN

NORAMET'S PARK AVENUE apartment was a swank place by the swankiest of standards, and since possession is nine-tenths of the law, it was dedicated to the exclusive use and enjoyment of the Chairman. Once the keys to the castle had been delivered to Fennell, they never again left his pocket.

The Noramet Board had been asked to approve the hefty capital expenditure on the basis that the apartment would accommodate visiting officers from out-of-state and would also provide a private facility for company social functions. Perhaps the Capital Appropriation Request was technically defensible, in that Fennell lived in Greenwich, Connecticut and was, technically speaking, an out-of-state officer. However, having approved the expenditure, most Noramet Directors would have been outraged to learn that Fennell was the only officer, in-state or out-of-state, to ever use the place. They would have been scandalized to learn that he used it as a love nest.

Happily for everyone, no outside Directors became outraged and scandalized, because only insiders knew that Fennell and his girlfriends had exclusive possession of the place. There are some things outside Directors should know. There are other things that would just upset them unnecessarily. Better to let sleeping Directors sleep.

Of course, the inside Directors of Noramet, along with a goodly number of Noramet staff, were in-the-know, and depending on gender, were either morally indignant or jealously indignant. However, their joint and several instincts for survival proved stronger than their righteous indignation, so they were silently indignant. To put it another way, everyone misplaced his or her whistle, so no one was able to blow the whistle.

Richard Fennell had bedded down in the Park Avenue apartment on Thursday night, having explained to his wife that a deal was brewing and that an evening meeting would preclude his commuting back to Connecticut. Elizabeth Fennell didn't believe him but didn't much care whether he was lying or not. Many years had passed since she'd last wondered or worried about her husband's infidelities; and many years had passed since he'd last troubled himself to invent elaborate fictions. Nowadays, his perfunctory excuses were made as a courtesy only, in order to avoid mix-ups in their Greenwich social calendar. There are some things wives should know; there are other things that would just upset them unnecessarily.

This time Fennell's excuse was partially true—a much higher truth quotient than usual. A deal was, in fact, brewing, and there had, in fact, been an evening meeting at the Commerce Club. What Fennell forgot to mention was the fact that he was also bedding his administrative assistant at the apartment.

Now it was Friday morning—the morning after.

Susan Blair was fast asleep in the master bedroom, the sweet untroubled sleep of youth. Fennell was wide awake in the study, the sour wakefulness of lost youth. He had been sitting there motionless for the better part of an hour, and although his eyes were shut fast, he was wide awake. A thick briefing binder lay unopened on the table beside him, unopened because all the information he needed was well-lodged in his remarkable memory. His mind was moving at lightning speed as it sliced and diced and analyzed the complex mass of financial data, business strategies, and human dynamics that comprised *Project Otter*. He had anticipated that Thorne Sullivan's overtures to Lunex would be rejected. What had surprised and infuriated him was Manetti's insolence. Manetti had thrown down the gauntlet, a challenge which Fennell couldn't ignore. Reminded of King Henry's response to the insolent Dauphin, he moved to the bookshelves and took down his well-thumbed volume of Shakespeare's plays. When he found the passage, he read it aloud ... and with feeling,

> *Scorn and defiance, slight regard, contempt*
> *And anything that may not misbecome*
> *The mighty sender doth he prize you at.*

Manetti was several hundred miles out of earshot, so Fennell's scorn and defiance only served to awaken Susan Blair. However, being a sweet and untroubled young woman, she rolled over and resumed her sweet untroubled sleep. For his part, Fennell returned to his leather throne and resumed his ruminations.

Mountain Lake would be his last acquisition and would crown an exceptional career. His last hurrah.

After *Project Otter,* he'd retire and Doyle would succeed him. Doyle couldn't replace him—no one could replace him—but Doyle was experienced and capable and ready for the top job. He deserved the top job, and Fennell would see that he got it. Fennell admired everything about Doyle, except for his humble origins, his night-school education, and his middle-class morality. It was bad enough to have humble origins and a night-school *alma mater*, but it was downright perverse to be proud of them, as Doyle was of his. He was a common man of high intelligence, a likeable plebeian to be sure but a plebeian nonetheless. Fennell reminded himself once again that the captains of industry are no longer recruited from the ranks of gentlemen, and that Doyle's background, or lack of same, would probably prove to be an asset rather than a liability. "Bring on the mongrels," he muttered to himself.

Fennell was reluctantly forced to admit that Doyle had strengths Fennell lacked. Whereas the rank-and-file at Noramet feared Fennell, they loved Doyle, a man of the people to whom they could and did relate. Fennell was, in fact, a thoughtful and generous CEO, but his thoughtfulness and generosity were anonymous, well hidden behind the scenes and behind his surrogates. He had never tried to reach down and touch the rank-and-file at Noramet; he'd never had a desire to do so, nor had he ever felt any compunction to do so. He was a Wall Street Coriolanus. In direct response to his patrician reserve, the Noramet troops had always stood aloof from him and resented him. He knew that, but he didn't care. Why should he care?

Although Doyle was Fennell's protégé, he and Doyle were business associates rather than friends. They arrived in the morning from different worlds and returned in the evening to different worlds. He had never invited the Doyles to Connecticut, nor had the Doyles ever invited the Fennells to New Jersey. Different worlds! Best not to mix business with friendship. Best to keep business associates at arm's length. Doyle was Fennell's preferred subordinate, but a subordinate nonetheless.

As Fennell sat ruminating, a nebulous foreboding kept nagging at him, a vague fear that unforeseen events might defeat Project Otter and might defeat him. In the final analysis, he had much more to lose than to win. If he won, the business world would greet his success with a yawn. Big Noramet was always expected to win. There would be no standing ovation; the applause would be muted and perfunctory. On the other hand, if he lost—if Lunex and/or Laurentian successfully fended off Noramet—that would be news indeed. Big time news.

If either of those Davids did manage to slay Goliath, Fennell's and Noramet's aura of invincibility would vanish overnight, and he would slink into retirement leaving a tarnished legacy behind.

He knew full well that his innate reserve, perceived as arrogance, had not endeared him to the media. He did not give ingratiating interviews. In fact, he seldom gave interviews at all. He had been so private and unapproachable for so long that the media would relish the spectacle of Goliath *"falling flat upon his face to the earth."* There would be a pandemic of *schadenfreude*. Should he risk it?

Except for Manetti's insolence, Fennell could be persuaded to give a pass to Mountain Lake. It was certainly an alluring prospect, but at the end of the day, it was not vital to Noramet's future, and acquiring Mountain Lake could become a messy affair. It was Manetti's damned insolence that tipped the scales. Damn Manetti! He was forcing Fennell to retaliate. Mountain Lake wasn't vital to Noramet's future—true enough—but it was still a prize worth fighting for. Crushing Manetti would be icing on the cake, and a very rich icing indeed. He reminded himself that he and Doyle had never lost a takeover battle, and they'd been in some tough ones. It was time to buckle on the armour and lead his troops into battle, one last time. He picked up the phone and punched in a number.

"Doyle," came the gruff voice.

"Project Otter looks like a go to me. I've slept on it."

And so has Susan Blair, thought Doyle.

"I've only got one reservation, Tim."

"What's that?"

"You! You've been dragging your ass on this one, right from the beginning. I want to know what's on your mind. It's decision time, so tell me what's been spooking you."

"Nothing really, or in any event, nothing rational. Project Otter looks do-able, although it will get expensive if Laurentian gets in the way."

"I think I've recruited Macdonald as our mole. If I'm right, and if he's right, we should know on Wednesday whether Laurentian will tender to a Noramet bid. If you have no rational concerns, what are your irrational ones?"

"Just my Irish gut."

"You and your Irish gut are out of fighting trim."

"Quite possibly. Maybe it's time for me to retire."

"That would rob me of the pleasure of firing you. I don't want your resignation. I want you to stop sounding like the Three Witches, because I'm starting to feel like Macbeth."

"Who'd he play for?" asked Doyle dryly.

"Come on, Tim! Come on! You know I won't press the *go* button unless and until you're on side. So apparently Project Otter stands or falls on you. If your Irish gut is rumbling about Manetti, forget it. I know you think Noramet did him wrong, and maybe I think so too, but all that happened decades ago. Business is war, and Project Otter is business."

"Perhaps Manetti sees it that way too."

"I don't give a damn how Manetti sees it. Pericatu is history, no matter how he sees it. Manetti is a nobody from nowhere, and I'm going to enjoy crushing the bastard. Now that we've exorcised that ghost, are there any other ghosts to deal with?"

"Just one, but it's more of a leprechaun than a ghost. You need some Irish to spot it, and just when you think you do spot it, it disappears again."

"Well, I've got no Irish in me, so you tell me what you see in your leprechaun's crystal balls."

"It's just idle speculation, which you'd neither like nor credit."

"I may not thank you, but I won't bite. Idle or not, let's hear your speculation. I insist."

"It's about a long-gone secretary of yours: Moira Fitzgerald."

"Long-gone indeed. What possible connection is there between Moira and Project Otter?"

"Moira resigned abruptly, back around nineteen eighty-seven or eight as I recall. Somewhere in there."

"She resigned, yes. I don't remember anything *abrupt* about it. We parted friends, as I recall."

"In that case I'm wrong, so let's skip it."

"No, go on! Let's assume she *resigned abruptly*. I'm curious to find out where your leprechaun is taking us."

"Warren Ransom resigned about a month after Moira left. Do you remember him?"

"Yes, and I know he's President and COO of Lunex now, if that's what you're getting at, but what's that got to do with Moira?"

"She's Mrs. Ransom."

There was a long pause before Fennell replied. "You should have told me."

"I only learned of it recently, and quite by accident."

"Who told you?"

"Isabel Robinson, another long-retired Noramet secretary. Do you remember her?"

"No. How can I be expected to remember former employees? Hell, I don't know half of our current employees."

"I met Isabel in New Jersey, on a train coming into Manhattan. We rode in together and reminisced about the good old days. Among her reminiscences was one to the effect that Moira and Warren Ransom had been secretly engaged for a couple of years before they left Noramet. She was a good friend of Moira and knew their big secret. She attended their wedding in Toronto."

"So where is your leaping leprechaun taking us?"

"I'm not sure, Dick. It seems curious to me that they both quit at the same time, quit good jobs, and slammed the door behind them, so to speak. We're getting close to the point where you're going to have to join the chase or abandon it."

"Keep going, Tim. I said I wouldn't bite you, and I won't. You're an Irish nuisance, but you're also the one person I can rely on."

"About a month after Moira resigned, you asked me to handle the severance arrangements in person, quietly and generously, so I did. That's how I got involved, and that's the only reason I got involved. Three things didn't compute. *One:* In the normal course, Human

Resources should have and would have done all the paperwork without my involvement. *Two:* Employees who voluntarily resign don't receive severance payments. *Three:* Somewhere along the way I learned, or at least got the impression, that you augmented the Noramet settlement with a personal cheque."

"And you've assumed all these years that I misconducted myself, that she quit in tears, and that I was buying her off. Is that what you've been thinking all these years?"

"I haven't been thinking about it 'all these years.' However, at the time, I thought it was something along those lines. Was I wrong?"

"Partly right and partly wrong; it's complicated."

"Look, Dick, I don't give a damn what happened. You asked me to explain my Irish gut, and I'm trying to do that. I'm concerned that your relationship with Moira, whatever that was, may have ramifications now."

"Our *relationship*, as you so delicately put it, consisted of one sexual encounter. It was a regrettable lapse, but it was also a consensual lapse. In any event, it's ancient history, just like Pericatu and Manetti are ancient history. Is your leprechaun telling you that Lunex will go to war to avenge Moira's honour? We're talking about a former secretary, not Helen of Troy."

"No, I doubt they'll go to war for Moira. In fact, I doubt anyone knows what happened, aside from Moira and you, and now me ... and perhaps Ransom. However, what if Ransom does know?"

"Then he'll hate my guts as much as Manetti hates my guts. Maybe more! Who cares? As to Moira, it wasn't rape; as to Ransom, he should have put a ring on her finger. Do you expect me to go to the Board and recommend that Noramet abandon Project Otter because of an indiscretion that occurred long, long ago? Do you want to prepare the slides for that presentation? I'm running a business, not writing a soap opera. Hold on, the other line's going."

As Fennell responded to the other call, Doyle reflected on the fact that he'd never ceased to admire Fennell's business acumen and connections but had long since ceased liking him as a person. However, the facts of life are the facts of life, and Doyle never forgot the fact that he owed his ascendancy at Noramet to Fennell and to Fennell alone. Fennell had picked him from the pack, and Fennell had the power to throw him back. The facts of life are the facts of life.

Fennell was back on the line. "I just told Matt to pick me up at nine fifteen, so I'd better get organized here. Look, Tim, in the course of human conduct, there has to be some statute of limitations on both corporate treachery and sexual romps, and surely a quarter century is a long enough limitation period. If Manetti and Moira are the only threats your leprechaun can conjure up, then I think we should go full bore and damn the torpedoes. As far as Manetti goes, I'm not a bit afraid of the bastard. I dislike him as much as he dislikes me. So, bugger Manetti. As to Moira, assuming she confessed all to Ransom, and assuming Ransom couldn't forgive her—two big assumptions—he wouldn't have married her in the first place, and/or he'd have come gunning for me years ago. Look Tim, if good girls go to Heaven, then bad boys go to Hell. So, I might as well enjoy my life on Earth. I've had many affairs in my life, as you well know, some of them with my secretaries, as you also know. If my every peccadillo had business consequences, then I'd have been out-of-business long ago. However, I've been a very successful CEO, so maybe womanizing is the key to success. Maybe you should try it. Maybe business schools should give courses in it. In any event, Moira is water under the bridge, and the river flows swiftly. Ransom may be girding for battle, but not because many years ago his then-fiancée was seduced by her boss."

"I thought you said it was consensual."

"It was a consensual seduction. Look, prurience is a concomitant of sex—great sex anyway—hence *consensual seduction*. It's past time you discovered that."

"If you say so."

"Save me from the Puritans! My dear Tim, these things happen, and that thing did happen. Whatever it was, it certainly wasn't rape. I'm sorry as hell it happened, sorrier than Moira, or you, or Moira's maiden aunt, but it did happen. It wouldn't have happened if she'd been wearing an engagement ring. My libido does observe the rules of the road. However, it did happen, many, many years ago, and the world has been moving on ever since. It did happen and we've got to move on too. So back to business! Project Otter will be good for Noramet—very good indeed—and I can't make Noramet shareholders pay for my past sins, real or imagined. So, quit jumping at shadows and let's go for the kill, like we have in the past. I smell blood! After we get Mountain Lake, I'll retire and repent my sins at leisure … and when you retire, you can repent my sins at leisure too." Without more, Fennell hung up.

CHAPTER
TWELVE

CONTRARY TO HIS bravado, Fennell was unnerved by his conversation with Doyle. He sat transfixed as his memory took charge of his mind and forced him to re-live that long-ago encounter with Moira Fitzgerald.

He remembered the cold November rains lashing Manhattan, horizontal sheets driven by raw and angry winds. He was in his office at Noramet Inc., confronting and admiring the raging elements as they beat furiously against his plate-glass fortress. It had amused him to think that his pre-historic ancestors would have taken to their clammy caves and cowered on such a day, whereas he was warm and dry and unafraid, standing nose to nose with the storm, daring the gods to strike the glass of champagne from his upraised hand.

Earlier that day, Noramet had taken over a competitor—swallowed it whole—in a less-than-friendly but not-quite-hostile merger. Noramet had become higher and mightier, and he, Vice President of Strategic Acquisitions, was feeling higher and mightier too.

It was Saturday afternoon. The carefully scripted closing ceremonies had taken place at noon in Noramet's board room. There had been the ritual signing of documents, the perfunctory handshakes, the fixed smiles, the feigned goodwill ("welcome aboard") and the forced camaraderie ("This is a win/win merger"). That done, the dissemblers had bolted *en masse* to salvage whatever was left of the weekend. Only he had stayed at the office, to savour his triumph in solitude. It was his triumph, for it was he who had quarterbacked the Noramet team to victory. One more in a series of successful acquisitions, one more step towards the CEO's office. It was in the stars. He was sure of it. He could taste it.

Then came a light knock on the door, followed by the appearance of his secretary's head.

"I'll be off now, Mr. Fennell, if you don't need me anymore."

"I thought you'd long gone, Moira. Everyone stampeded out of here a good half hour ago. No, I don't need you anymore, unless you'd like to join me in a toast to our success. You're an important player on the team, and we've all had to work overtime to win this one. Come and have a glass of champagne! Come and admire the storm! Then I won't need you anymore."

He poured a glass and carried it to her, but she kept her hands on the half-open door. "No thanks, really. Champagne doesn't always agree with me, particularly on an empty stomach, and I have an engagement tonight."

"So do I, but it's only two thirty. Is there a car waiting for you downstairs?"

"A subway car."

"Subway cars don't count. Albert's waiting for me in the garage, and now he's waiting for you, and he's faster than the subway. He'll whisk you home in jig time, after we've toasted our success and applauded all this Donner and Blitzen. This is a five-star storm, and we have dress-circle seats."

He took her arm and drew her into the office. She self-consciously accepted the glass and sat in her usual chair, as if to take dictation. He moved behind her and swiveled the chair so that she was facing the windows, and for a while, they admired the pyrotechnics in silence.

Why had he yielded to temptation? No doubt, it was the heady blend of Dom Perignon and business triumph. He knelt behind her chair and kissed the back of her neck. Startled and embarrassed, she stood up and moved away. Still kneeling, he raised both hands in a gesture of apology—a silent apology meant to convey that she was no longer in danger from him. From the neck up, it had been a sincere apology, but an erection has a mind of its own and no scruples.

Moira Fitzgerald had been his administrative assistant for over four years, during which time he had been unfailingly correct and formal, not only because their relationship should stay strictly professional but also because she was a very attractive young woman to whom he was very attracted. He reminded himself that Moira was his secretary, and that he must not abandon his scrupulous practice of de-personifying his secretaries. He reminded himself that he must not cross the dangerous threshold that leads from office friendship to personal friendship. Friendship be damned! He wanted her as a sex partner, not a friend. The game was on.

As if nothing had happened, he crossed to the side board and refilled their glasses. Then he saluted the gilt-framed portrait behind his desk. "To Gordon Robertson, my mentor, my friend, and the best chairman this company ever had."

She sat down again and compliantly raised her glass to the stern face in the frame.

"Gordon Robertson retired before you joined us, Moira, retired to Palm Beach. I haven't seen him recently, although he phones every couple of weeks. One of his better decisions was to recruit me; I'm sure you agree."

"Absolutely."

"Good, I thought you would. I was just thinking that it's dangerous for co-workers to be friends, so maybe we shouldn't be friends. What do you think?"

"You're the boss," she'd replied with a smile.

"That's a clever evasion, young lady. I've kept you longer than I said I would, and I apologize. Albert's waiting."

He wished she hadn't come, but she had come. He wished she'd stayed out of harm's way, but she hadn't. As she moved towards the door, he stepped forward and embraced her. It's true that she struggled and protested, but it's also true that she didn't scratch and scream. He carried her to the couch and undressed her gently. It's true that she continued to struggle and protest, but it's also true that she was sexually aroused.

They had sex—enthusiastic sex—beginning on the couch but ending on the floor, a good fifteen feet from the couch. Then he was rocking her gently in his arms. "Love in the teeth of a gale. If that ain't hubris, I don't know what is. I hope the gods weren't watching."

"I'm more concerned about mortals barging in here," she murmured drowsily.

"I flipped the lock, so no mortals can disturb us. I flipped the lights, so no one can see us—no one but the gods. If the gods are watching, do you think they're angry at us?"

"Yes, you've been mooning them."

She slept in his arms for a good half hour before rousing herself, collecting her clothes, and repairing to the en suite bathroom. He lay splayed on the rug in a state of euphoric collapse, listening to the rain beating against the windows and the muffled sound of the bathroom shower. He'd always fallen easily into lust, and he'd fallen again, big time. He lay there until he heard the shower stop; then he shambled to his feet and got dressed.

To his chagrin, the demure girl who returned to the office wasn't the lover who had left it. To his chagrin, she was his secretary again, altered and distant. To his chagrin, she looked pale and self-conscious. To his chagrin, there were tears in her eyes.

He hesitated for an instant and then moved to embrace her, but she avoided him and moved to the door. He wanted to detain her, but she was obviously bent on fleeing. Obviously ill-at-ease. He thought he could talk to her on the way to the car, but there were people on the elevator to the lobby. They rode in silence.

A security guard was on the elevator from the lobby to the garage. They rode in silence.

When they reached the garage, there were people milling around, and then his driver appeared. Fennell held the car door and said he'd call her, but he couldn't say more. He instructed Albert to drive her home and then return for him.

CHAPTER
THIRTEEN

FRIDAY EVENING WAS rainswept and muggy, a gloomy start to the Labour Day weekend.

Around eight o'clock, a silver Mercedes coupé wheeled smoothly into the driveway of a down-at-the-heels garage. The building was conspicuously rundown, not yet derelict but definitely decrepit, a structure of peeling paint and lost hope, a structure which was definitely out-of-place and out-of-spirit on this North Toronto street of starter homes. The exuberantly luxurious car was also out-of-place and out-of-spirit in a neighbourhood of SUVs.

Although the building (known to the neighbours as the *Depot*) was the size and shape of a three-bay commercial service station, the blistered clapboard facade was unbroken by garage doors, garage windows, or garage signs. Except for a mean little door (which had been incised at one corner of the building), and except for its municipal address (three metal numbers screwed into the face of that mean little door), the place was entirely anonymous.

Since the entire neighbourhood was zoned *single family residential*, except for the Depot, which was zoned *commercial*, the Depot was definitely a cow amongst the sheep. However, zoning is zoning, and the Depot had just as much right to conduct business in its commercial premises as the young couples had to cohabit in their residential premises.

If truth be told, it was not the Depot's commercial activity that unsettled the neighbours but rather the absence of same; things were always quiet at the Depot, much too quiet. Although the neighbours all carried on their baby-making activities behind closed curtains and behind closed doors, they resented the fact that the Depot also operated behind closed curtains and behind closed doors.

Speculation was rampant.

The only person seen coming to and going from the anonymous building came and went at irregular hours, wore jeans and a beard, drove an unmarked van, and never received customers on the premises. He looked like a drug dealer should look and acted like a drug dealer should act, so *faut de mieux*, he must be a drug dealer, and the building must be a drug depot.

Since the bearded stranger usually came and went during the day, it fell to the stay-at-home moms to do the spying. Although it wasn't for lack of trying, none of them had been able to spy anything through the dirty and heavily-curtained windows on the side walls of the Depot, nor had anyone been able to engage the bearded young man in conversation, apart from his ever-cheerful concurrence in anyone's weather observations. He always came and went by the little front door, and he always closed the door behind him, thus denying young mothers a peek-in.

There should be a law against ignoring your neighbours and minding your own business, but alas, there isn't.

The Mercedes announced itself with two impatient blasts of the horn, a din which brought several vigilant neighbours to their windows. However, it being Friday evening of a long weekend, the neighbourhood spy-watch had been reduced to a corporal's guard, and the few spies who were around were all sheltering indoors from the rain. They concluded, and reported, that the flashy coupé was there for a drug pickup.

After waiting a couple of minutes, the car announced itself again, this time with three sharp blasts—an outburst of automotive temper that brought the drug dealer to the door. He both acknowledged and dismissed the rude summons by clapping hands to ears and then shutting the door again. In a few minutes, he reappeared and began locking the door, a laborious process that involved no fewer than three locks—further proof to the flickering-curtain set that he was indeed a drug dealer, if not something worse.

Tonight, the bearded young man was wearing an oversized trench coat and carrying a large documents case. As he approached, the car trunk yawned open, a silent instruction to stow the case there. He did so, slammed the trunk rather too hard, and then slid into the passenger seat. "Filthy night!" he said, extending his hand. "I'm Walter Herrington. I assume you're Ross Macdonald."

Macdonald nodded, and they shook hands.

"Your car has lots of horn," observed Herrington, a quiet rebuke that Macdonald ignored.

"You're all muffled up," said Macdonald dismissively. "Aren't you hot?"

"Yes, but the rain gives me an excuse to wear it. It's a bit of a disguise."

"The only people I see carrying those fat cases are fat accountants," retorted Macdonald. "Are you disguising yourself as a fat accountant?"

"I look like an accountant, do I? I sort of thought I looked like a lawyer."

Macdonald turned south on Mount Pleasant Road and headed downtown. Several minutes passed before Herrington broke the silence. "Nice wheels!"

Macdonald responded with a bored shrug, it being beneath his dignity to acknowledge the niceness of his wheels. "Do you have everything you need?" he asked.

"Everything we talked about on the phone."

Macdonald grunted sceptically. "This has to be *strictly confidential.*"

"Everything I do is strictly confidential," replied Herrington, realizing that his unfavourable first impression of Ross Macdonald had ripened into an unfavourable second impression. "That's why I do my own work."

Macdonald responded with another sceptical grunt. "Three thousand, right?"

"Right."

"I suspect you're robbing me, but I haven't got time to shop around. I'm going to make it four thousand."

"If the price had been four thousand, I'd have said four thousand," replied Herrington. "I don't negotiate, up or down, and I don't accept tips."

"Yes, but I want more than strict confidentiality. I want amnesia. I want you to forget you ever did this job. I want you to forget you ever met me. No invoices. No records. That's why I'm paying you in cash, and that's why I'm paying you the extra thousand."

"Look, the fee includes strict confidentiality, unless and until I get arrested. When the equipment is installed and working, you pay me three thousand cash. If and when I get my stuff back, you get five hundred back. That's what we agreed, and that's what I expect."

Although he was accustomed to administering rebukes, Macdonald was unaccustomed to receiving them. However, he could check his temper when necessary, and it was necessary to check his temper now. He expressed his irritation by inserting a CD and turning up the volume.

Since they had lost no time in establishing mutual antipathy, they were both happy to ride in silence and let Diana Krall seduce them.

Macdonald didn't re-open the conversation until he was pulling into his parking spot under First Canadian Place. "There shouldn't be anybody in the office tonight," he said. "Even the target takes Friday nights off. However, if anybody is there, we'll have to beat a retreat." He paused, "I won't be identifying the target, so don't ask and don't get curious."

"I'm not the least bit curious," replied Herrington, who almost added *'you prick.'* "The less I know the better for me, so I only ask what I need to know."

There was no further discussion until they were inside the Laurentian offices. "You seem familiar with this building," said Macdonald.

"I've done work in all the downtown office towers."

Macdonald left Herrington in the reception area while he made a quick tour of the floor. Then he led the way to his office.

"No one working overtime?" asked Herrington.

"No, I figured every one of those lazy bastards would be gone, and I was right."

"Gone on Friday night of a long weekend! They sure are lazy bastards," said Herrington, as he removed a piece of equipment from the case. "Where does this receiver go?"

Macdonald opened the bottom drawer of his desk. "This desk locks, and I've got the keys."

Herrington carefully positioned the receiver. "I could force that drawer in two seconds and pick that lock in two minutes."

"Good for you! Do you have a better idea?"

Herrington shrugged. "It's your office."

"And this is my idea. The desk stays locked, and I have the keys. This office is locked after hours, and my dragon secretary guards the door when I'm not here."

"Let's hope you have the only keys. Anyway, lay a file folder on top of the receiver, so it's out of sight at first glance. Which office gets mic'ed?"

"Next door."

Herrington took off his trench coat and tossed it over a chair. Now he was dressed like a telephone repairman, complete with a Bell Canada logo on his shirt.

"Is that your super-bugger costume?"

Herrington ignored the sneer and removed a steel tool box from the documents case. Then he moved to the door.

"Hang on!" said Macdonald, "I'd better go with you."

"No, I prefer to work alone; and if someone shows up, it makes more sense if I'm alone in there. Also, what goes for me goes for you; the less you know the better you can lie."

Macdonald didn't reply but was thinking how much he'd like to hire the cocky little bastard, so he could have the pleasure of firing the cocky little bastard.

Herrington was back in half an hour. "That's one hell of an office. Bigger than yours. Okay, let's test the system. Go next door and walk all around, speaking as you go. Speak as if you were having a normal conversation and be sure to sit in every chair, particularly the desk chair. In about three minutes, I'll phone you to see how well we're picking up the telephone conversations."

Macdonald went to the next office, picked up a copy of Laurentian's annual report and began reading it aloud as he moved about the room. The telephone rang, and he had a short conversation with Herrington before returning to his own office. Then Herrington switched on the recorder, and they listened to the replay.

"That's not too bad," was all Macdonald offered, although he was astonished by the audibility of the tape.

"That's damn good!" said Herrington. "The mic's are voice-activated, so the tape starts whenever there's a voice in the room and stops when there's silence. If Mr. Drake talks to himself—"

"I told you not to get curious."

"And I told you I'm not the lease bit curious; his name's on the door. As I was saying, if Mr. Drake talks to himself, you'll go through a lot of tapes, so make sure you change cassettes before they run out. There are twelve cassettes in that box. If you haven't picked up useful information on a tape, just press the erase button, which will rewind the tape. You can start by erasing the test."

Macdonald handed over an envelope. "Three thousand, since that's all you want." Herrington quickly checked the contents, dropped the envelope into the tool box, deposited the tool box in the documents case, and donned his trench coat.

Mission accomplished, the co-conspirators quietly left the premises without leaving a trace of their visit behind ... or so they thought.

When they reached the street level, Herrington took his leave. "I have another downtown appointment. Friday nights are busy nights for fat accountants. Give me a call when you're ready to have the place de-bugged. Like I told you on the phone, the sooner the better; less time, less risk. And remember, the only link to you is the receiver in your desk. If you get spooked about anything, anything at all, remove the receiver from your office. You've got my number."

CHAPTER
FOURTEEN

LONG WEEKENDS SEEM to slip away more quickly than two-day weekends, and the Labour Day weekend was history. Now it was September, with summer on the wane.

It was just past nine o'clock on Tuesday morning when Drake's telephone rang. He made a face when he saw Ross Macdonald's number on the screen. "Alastair, can we have a word about the Lunex business?"

"I thought we had."

"Last Wednesday, yes, but only briefly. I've been giving it further thought, and I'd like to give you my considered views."

"I think I know your views, Ross, and as I said before, I invite you to express them at tomorrow's Board meeting. However, if you have something else to say, then come along now."

When Drake received someone in his office, he customarily moved from his desk to the chesterfields, a courteous attempt to put the visitor at ease. As Macdonald entered, Drake stayed put at his desk, thus signalling that this visit was an interruption and that he expected the interruption to be short. "Well, Ross, to review the bidding, you think we should tender our Lunex shares to the Noramet bid, if and when the Noramet bid materializes. On the other hand, I think Laurentian should aim at a friendly merger with

Lunex and should give serious consideration to trying to block a Noramet takeover bid. I haven't changed my views. Have you?"

"No, but I want to emphasize one aspect—an aspect we overlook at our peril."

"The floor is yours, provided you can emphasize it in ten minutes; I have a meeting coming up. I doubt you'll change my mind, and I doubt I'll change yours, but let's hear what you've got to say … as long as it's not a rehash of our previous discussions."

"I have a concern, a grave concern, that if Laurentian gets in Noramet's way, Noramet may turn its sights on us," said Macdonald. "If we become the target, we're bare ass to the wind. We've got no big-brother shareholder who'll be a white knight for us. I don't know why you want to play with fire, particularly when a juicy takeover premium will be ripe for the picking."

"Perhaps because a Laurentian/Lunex merger makes good business sense to me. I firmly believe Mountain Lake will prove to be what Rocco Manetti calls 'a once-in-a-lifetime discovery,' and I firmly believe that Laurentian should revisit its strategic decision to abandon gold. That's what I'm going to tell our Directors tomorrow. In my view, we've got the inside track on something gigantic, and I'm going to say that to the Board. I agree with Rocco that opportunity is hammering on our door, and we should have the vision and courage to seize that opportunity. And don't forget that those Mountain Lake properties were Laurentian claims just a few years ago. That will be my message to the Board."

"If Mountain Lake's all that good, we can *seize the opportunity* by exchanging our Lunex shares for Noramet shares. Let Noramet develop Mountain Lake, and we can take a free ride."

"What self-respecting mining company looks for a free ride? A free ride in the back seat! I don't think we should back down to a bully. I don't think we should cut and run under threat. Rocco Manetti wants to see Mountain Lake through to production, and so do I. I've never seen Rocco so excited about anything, and he's not the excitable type."

"Don't forget we sold those claims to Lunex because we didn't want them."

"We invested in Rocco Manetti and his team of geologists, and we've been well rewarded for so doing. Let's stick with a winner. Why let Noramet take Lunex off the board just to feed Richard Fennell's insatiable appetite for acquisitions?"

"Do you know Fennell?" asked Macdonald.

"Only by reputation. He's reputed to be a ruthless operator, and his track record seems to validate his reputation. Do you know him?"

"Never met the man, but I doubt he's as bad as his reputation. Are you anti-American, Alastair?"

"No, I'm anti-corporate megalomaniacs of any nationality. As far as the Americans go, our real enemy is Ottawa—the enemy within—which hasn't got the vision and guts to protect Canada's natural resources. Our real enemies are the spineless provincial premiers, with a few exceptions."

"I thought you were a free trader," said Macdonald.

Drake shrugged. "You can be a free trader without giving away the farm. A baby smiles when you steal its candy, and our retarded government smiles as Canada's natural resources get stolen away, not knowing what they had, not knowing what they've lost."

"You and I aren't on the same page, Alastair."

"It's okay to be on different pages, so speak your mind tomorrow. For all I know, you may even be on the right page. If Laurentian were to lock horns with Noramet, we could very well become the dinner and not the diner. I hadn't overlooked that possibility, and I concede that's a foreseeable risk."

"More of a probability than a possibility, and since our stock is undervalued, Noramet would be sitting down to an inexpensive dinner."

"Laurentian has never run scared in the past, and I don't propose to start running scared now. If it made sense for us to get out of the gold business when we did, then in my view, it makes a lot more sense to get back into the gold business now. Anyway, stick to your guns! Our job is to present honest analysis to the Directors, fully and fairly. Their job is to decide whether or not to duke it out with Noramet. Just so I fully understand your position, do you have any other concerns?"

"Yes, Manetti himself is a concern. A merger of Laurentian and Lunex would be a marriage from hell; the two cultures are incompatible."

"In what way?"

"In every way. Take the Lunex offices for example; they resemble a site trailer at a field camp. That concern may seem trivial to you, but their offices are a reflection of Manetti's attitudes. He's intentionally out-of-step with everyone else on Bay Street, and he likes it that way. He dresses like a prospector in the bush, and so do the rest of the Lunex gang. Casual dress is one thing, but plaid shirts and bush pants are another. I don't object to the dress code as much as the sneering attitude implicit in the dress code."

"I don't think he's sneering," said Drake. "It's his way of keeping the Lunex people focussed on their core business, which as you point out, is exploration. Anyway, if we were to merge companies, we wouldn't merge offices or dress codes. As I foresee it, Lunex would stay exactly where it is now, plaid shirts and all ... a separate and distinct unit of Laurentian. Besides, Ross, I bet you look dashing in a plaid shirt. The Macdonald tartan."

"Yes, I do ... at the cottage. Look, Alastair, if Manetti were to become part of the Laurentian management team, I guarantee you'd lose some key people around here. You may regard him as a giant in the mining industry, but others, like me, think he's a rebel without a cause."

"If I didn't know you better, I might think you felt threatened. Do you feel threatened, Ross?"

"Personally? Not a bit! But he'd be bad news for Laurentian."

"He's been good news for Lunex; he's kept a crack team together over there. As you know, I've been a Director of Lunex for several years now, so I've had ample opportunity to watch him in action. Frankly, I'm envious of the unswerving loyalty and respect he engenders. Do you think you and I command that kind of unswerving loyalty and respect around here? He's independent, somewhat short-tempered, and perhaps a trifle eccentric, but I wouldn't call him a rebel. He's his own man, but so are you, and so am I. Different personalities, that's all."

"That doesn't alter my view that he'd be a disruptive influence around Laurentian."

"Well, then, we agree to disagree. We'll discuss all the pros and cons at tomorrow's meeting and then let the Directors decide." Drake smiled, as if to himself. "If it's any comfort, I can assure you that Rocco Manetti won't be on Laurentian's management team while I'm still here."

"That's all well and good, but you won't be here in a few months."

"Tell me more." Drake let Macdonald twist in the wind for a long moment before he continued. "I don't recall saying anything about leaving in a few months."

"I must have misunderstood." Macdonald's face was scarlet.

"Misunderstood what? Or whom?"

"I don't remember who told me... Just a stupid rumour, I guess." Macdonald extracted a handkerchief and mopped his brow. "Rumours fly around here all the time, as you well know, and the CEO is always the favourite target. Anyway, I'm glad the rumour is false."

"You don't look glad; you look flustered."

"I'm troubled that someone at Laurentian would circulate a false rumour like that, and that I'd believed it."

"So am I. You could have asked me about it."

"I didn't want to intrude. I assumed you'd tell me what and when you wanted me to know."

"Yes, I guess that's a fair assumption. If you remember who's spreading rumours, please let me know. If he's a rumour monger, I'll fire him. If he's a soothsayer, I'll hire him."

Macdonald returned to his own office and shut the door. He stood at the window, pondering his next moves as he gazed down at the toy cars inching along King Street. Blurting out Drake's plans for early retirement had been a stupid slip, and Drake was obviously suspicious of his rather lame explanation. What game was Drake playing? Just a few hours ago, he'd told his daughter-in-law that he was going to announce his retirement in February. Had Macdonald misheard the tape? He locked his office door, unlocked his desk, and then rewound the tape until he located the right place. It was Drake's voice, loud and clear.

"You and John can quit nagging me. I've decided to retire."

"I'm so pleased, Alastair. I know we've been nagging you, but the job has been wearing you down, and we've been worried. It's not been the same since Beth died. When are you going to pack it in?"

"I'll announce it in February, to take effect in April ... after the Annual Meeting. Tell John but no one else. I've got a few things I have to straighten out before I go, and I'll be a lame-duck chairman if this gets out."

"Of course! We'll say nothing..."

Macdonald switched off; he had no interest in re-hearing the latest accomplishments of Drake's grandchildren. It was clear to him that the things Drake had to "straighten out" referred to a merger with Lunex. Of course, Manetti wouldn't be joining Laurentian's management team as long as Drake was around, since Drake was about to retire, and Drake had tagged Manetti to succeed him.

He punched in Bill Graydon's number and waited a long minute while Graydon's secretary put the call through. "Ross! How are you doing?"

"Not great. I promised Dick I'd call you when I found out how the wind was blowing around here."

"Right. How's she blowing?"

"Cold! As I told you, there's a Board meeting tomorrow, and it looks like Drake's going to pitch the white-knight option."

There was a long silence. "Did you raise the prospect of a Noramet bid for Laurentian?" asked Graydon.

"Yes, but he was there already."

"What did he say?"

"He said Laurentian doesn't run scared."

"So, he's *stubborn tough*. Okay! We can handle that. You'll be at the meeting, I presume."

"Of course."

"And you'll be opposing Drake's recommendations."

"Vigorously! And Drake knows I will. The meeting isn't until two o'clock, so I've got a few hours to lobby behind the scenes. I think I can influence a few of our Directors."

"That's the ticket, Ross. A word here, a word there… Get them thinking in the right direction."

"I'll give you a call tomorrow evening … let you know what the Board decides."

"I'll be travelling tomorrow, so why don't you call Dick at the New York number I gave you. I'll call him Thursday and get the news."

CHAPTER
FIFTEEN

IT WAS TUESDAY night at ten o'clock on the dot. O'Malley's rust-splotched car turned into the designated lot and parked in the open, well away from other cars. With visions of cash dancing in his head, O'Malley intended to be punctual and easy to find. He turned up the volume on his favourite rock station, cracked open a bottle of Seagrams VO, and settled back to wait.

Almost half an hour passed before Manetti stealthily approached the car and grabbed O'Malley's shoulder through the open window.

"Geez!" shouted O'Malley. "You damn near scared the piss out of me. Geez! I didn't see you sneakin' up. So, where's your car?"

"Pierrette has it. She dropped me off at my office, and I walked back."

"You should have brought her along."

"To meet my blackmailer? To look at the photographs?"

"Geez, Rocco, don't take it personal-like. We're partners, eh? I'd sure like to see *la belle Pierrette* again; she was a good-lookin' girl. Hell, I wouldn't have said nothin' about them pichers in front of her."

"Well, *la belle Pierrette* thinks I'm working late, and she's en route to Muskoka."

"*Muskoka?* Helluva time for a woman to be drivin' north on her own, if you ask me."

"I didn't ask you."

"She's probably glad to get away from you, eh?"

"You're probably right. She also has to meet a contractor in the morning."

"Wha' for?"

"You're a curious fellow in more ways than one. We're having some work done on the cottage. Okay?"

"It's okay by me. Do you believe her?"

Ignoring the remark, Manetti circled the car and slipped into the passenger seat. "Let's get down to business." He handed over an envelope. "Eighteen hundred; do you want to count it?"

"C'mon! Wha'dya take me for, Rocco? I trust you. Like I said, we're partners, eh?"

"Unfortunately, yes. Partners in crime. I brought along a bottle of *Balvenie* to seal the partnership deal ... but maybe you don't want to switch whiskies."

O'Malley reached across and snatched the bottle. "Don't mind tradin' up," he said, pulling the cork and taking a generous slug. "I'm gonna take some of what's in this envelope and get me a case of *Balvenie*." He gestured down the road towards the Queen's Quay liquor store.. "Last time I was in there, a couple of them likker-store bastards threw me out on my keester. Accused me of shopliftin'."

"Were you?"

"Yes and no, you might say. Anyway, next time, I'll make one of them flunkies carry a case of *Balvenie* out for me and put it in my trunk. Then I'll tip him a loonie. Fuck 'em!"

"The Scotch would be worth more than the car. You'd do better to invest your ill-gotten gains in some new wheels."

"Maybe I will when you set up that annuity thing for me. I like that, eh? When will it start?"

"I told you, it'll take two or three weeks. Then I'll expect to get *all* the photographs, right?"

"Sure! Sure! Most of them anyway."

"We discussed that last Wednesday. It's all or none. It's all or nothing. Once the annuity's up and running, you'll be fully covered. You won't need the photographs anymore."

"Most likely not, most likely not ... but you never know what's down the road. I mean, thirty-six grand's fine for now, Rocco, but you never know what's down the road." He took on some more Scotch. "Put yourself in my shoes, eh? You're all I've got. I'd be crazy to let you off the hook. For starters, what about inflation?"

"For starters, what about the deal we made?"

"The annuity thing is fine, Rocco. I like it. But I need an insurance policy. Nothin' personal, eh? I won't make a nuisance of mysehlf. Nothin' like that. But I need an inshurance polishy." He aimed a drunkard's grin in the general direction of Manetti. "Anyway, Rocco, how would you know if I gave you all them pichers? How would you know, eh?"

"You're right. I wouldn't, which is why I'll make arrangements to have you murdered if ever you double cross me. Just like I told you last Wednesday. *Capisce?*"

"*Murdered?* Get real Rocco! You wouldn't do that."

"Double cross me and find out."

"Geez, Rocco, we're old hockey buddies, eh? You don't threaten to kill an old hockey buddy. Geez, you can trush me." O'Malley's head slumped on his chest, as he lapsed into a drunken coma.

Manetti's first impulse was to abandon him there, but he quickly concluded that it was too risky for both of them. He got out of the car, and with much difficulty, dragged the hulk across to the passenger side. That done, he pushed O'Malley into a more or less sitting position and closed the door to prop him there.

As Manetti slid behind the wheel, he glanced nervously around, wondering who'd been watching the show. If there were any witnesses, they were invisible to him. Appropriate to the occasion, a Scotch mist was shrouding the parking lot, so maybe there weren't any witnesses.

During his ungentle eviction from the driver's seat, O'Malley had kept a death grip on the open bottle, thus causing most of the whisky to flood his trousers. Drunk he was, but incontinent he wasn't. Even Paddy couldn't piss forty proof. Had he been conscious, this shameful waste of fine Scotch would have elicited a scream of anguish, but he was unconscious and thus suffered no angst.

Manetti was unconcerned about the spilled Scotch, except that Scotch fumes filled the car and would fill the nostrils of any traffic cop who came within thirty feet of the car. He lifted O'Malley's Scotch-sodden wallet from his Scotch-sodden back pocket, found his address, and tossed the clammy wallet onto the back seat. "Come on, you blackmailing drunk, I'll drive you home."

Manetti weighed the respective merits of several routes, but none of them guaranteed safe passage. He drove to the exit, but there he stopped, wondering which way to turn. He took a long look at O'Malley, slumped against the passenger door and dead to the world—a scene guaranteed to attract the attention of any passing police cruiser. What would he tell the cops if he were stopped? What would the drunk babble, if roused from his stupor and questioned? How would he or the drunk explain an envelope with eighteen one-hundred-dollar bills? He reached into O'Malley's jacket and retrieved the envelope. "Just till we get you home," he explained aloud, but Sleeping Ugly was blissfully unaware that his pockets had been picked yet again.

Manetti began to worry that O'Malley might have incriminating photographs on his person or in the car, photographs which would show up during a police search. He began to realize with horror that this evening might be a prelude to the rest of his life, a puppet show in which he would be the puppet and a drunken clown would be the puppet master.

A police cruiser drove slowly east along Queen's Quay, and as if reading Manetti's thoughts, the cop stared hard at the Escort as he passed. Manetti instinctively headed in the opposite direction, but as he swung west onto Queen's Quay, he spotted another police cruiser parked down the block. Responding to instinct again, he abruptly swerved onto an unlit pier that jutted into Lake Ontario. It was dark there, but was it safe from prying eyes? Even if no police had seen the car enter the *No Entry* driveway, they must surely patrol the pier from time to time. If only he could get O'Malley on his feet and moving, he could get him home by cab. There were lots of cabs cruising Queen's Quay, and the police wouldn't be curious about two passengers in a taxi. Then he'd come back and retrieve the car.

"Time to go home!" He shook O'Malley by the shoulders, but O'Malley didn't respond. "Wake up, you drunken slob!" O'Malley didn't hear the insult. Manetti punched him smartly in the rib cage and then punched him there again. It was the second punch that raised the drunkard's consciousness quotient from drunken coma to semi-conscious stupor, and which elicited an outpouring of slurred obscenities.

Assuming O'Malley was now conscious, Manetti went around and opened the passenger door, whereupon the drunk toppled headfirst to the roadway. Although Manetti managed to partially break the fall, O'Malley cracked his head on the pavement, a sobering experience for any drunk. Awake now, but disoriented, he lurched to his feet and began cursing Manetti, who was trying to help him up. O'Malley pushed him away angrily and staggered down the pier, holding a whisky-soaked handkerchief to his bleeding temple—a single-malt antiseptic pad which even the toniest private clinics couldn't afford.

As Manetti followed him, O'Malley kept backing away, assuming in his confusion that Manetti had knocked him to the ground in the first place and intended to do so again.

"Come on, O'Malley! I'll call a taxi and take you home."

"Fuck off, you *wop bastard!* The price just went up on them pichers!"

"Time to go home! We'll talk about the pictures tomorrow."

"Fuck you, you *wop bastard!* We'll talk about them right now!"

"Don't call me a wop bastard, O'Malley. I'm warning you. If you're sober enough to say it, you're sober enough to know what you're saying. Now let's get a taxi."

"Sure, I know what I'm shayin', *wop bastard*. I'll call you anythin' I like, and I like *wop bastard*." Then he began shouting loudly. "Hey, everybody! Listen up! I've got shome pichers to shell. They're worth double the thirty-six thoushen this wop bastard is offerin' to—"

O'Malley took the punch full in the mouth but didn't feel any pain. He staggered backwards, and then he was briefly in free fall. There was a rush of water which filled his nostrils and swallowed him up.

CHAPTER
SIXTEEN

JACK SEAGRAM WAS a Jack-of-all-trades at Laurentian, an officer-at-large who handled special assignments. He enjoyed a special status in the Company because he had no status, because no one quite knew what he did, and more importantly, because he reported to the Chairman and *only* to the Chairman. He was untouchable.

Notwithstanding his taciturn manner, Jack Seagram was happy in his work. What he particularly valued about the job was his complete independence from bureaucratic interference. He was a greying field geologist who had come in from the cold, and who harboured a thinly-disguised contempt for Head Office denizens, few of whom could pitch a tent in an organized campground, let alone the wilderness.

Since everyone in a corporation gets a title, whether he or she needs a title or wants a title, even Jack Seagram couldn't escape labelling. When the Vice President of Human Resources consulted him about a suitable title, Seagram said, "*Call me Ahab and fuck off; I'm busy.*" The long-suffering Vice President wasn't foolhardy enough to pick a fight with the untouchable Jack Seagram, so he consulted his organizational thesaurus and came up with a proper title: *Director of Special Projects.*

On Wednesday evening, Drake telephoned Seagram at home. "Jack, when was the last time you had the offices checked for bugging devices?"

"April. I have a security firm sweep the place twice a year. April, just before the Annual Meeting, and October."

"All the offices?"

"Yes."

"Could you get your security firm to do a sweep tomorrow evening without anyone knowing?"

"Sure. The coast should be clear by eight. The whole three floors?"

"No, just my office. Call me at home when they're finished. If they find anything, don't let them go until we've talked."

"Sure."

"Suppose they found a bug. I assume they'd also find out who's doing the snooping?"

"They're the best in the business," replied Seagram. "What's up?"

"Probably nothing, Jack. Probably nothing at all. I'm probably suffering from paranoia."

"Better than diarrhea. Anything I should know?"

"Two things, but I'm only going to tell you one of them. I'm left-handed, so I have my phone on the left-hand side of my desk. When I took my first call Tuesday morning, the phone set was out of position. A right-handed person sitting at my desk would be inclined to reposition the phone the way I found it."

"Probably a right-handed cleaning woman calling home. Sitting at the Chairman's desk to scold her kids would give her extra authority. Anyway, everybody has to sign in and out on the weekends, so I'll check with Building Security. That's all you want to tell me, right?"

"Right. If it's just paranoia, I'd prefer not to parade my neuroses, and if it's for real, you'll find out for yourself."

"When did you discover whatever it is you don't want to tell me?"

"That was on Tuesday too ... more of a suspicion than a discovery. I know you're thinking that I should have got you on the job sooner."

"Well, I'm on the job now."

"With respect to the coast being clear, the coast *won't* be clear if Ross Macdonald is still in the office."

Seagram raised his eyebrows, but his voice didn't betray his surprise. "Understood," he said.

CHAPTER
SEVENTEEN

SINCE O'MALLEY WAS pretty well anaesthetized before the punch, he hadn't felt the punch. Manetti lunged forward to save him and did manage to grab one of his arms, but O'Malley's backward momentum couldn't be arrested. Manetti shrugged off his jacket and crouched at the edge of the pier, staring intently at the black water, poised to dive in when O'Malley's head surfaced. The flotsam-specked water lapped gently against the pilings, but no head surfaced.

After a while, Manetti stopped crouching and sat down, his legs dangling over the edge. Wherever O'Malley was, he was beyond rescue. Manetti continued to scan the water, waiting now for the police to come, not knowing what to say when they did. He mused that there had been neither bang nor whimper at O'Malley's passing … just a dull splash. However, he'd been shouting blue murder just prior to the splash. Surely someone must have called the police or alerted somebody.

As Manetti waited, he drifted into the past, his mind churning and spinning as he relived that July afternoon in 1974. He had relived that day countless times before and would relive it countless times thereafter.

He saw his rattletrap Fiat bumping painfully along an abandoned logging road, the little car being called on to function as an all-terrain vehicle, and at the same time being forced to bear aloft a roof-mounted canoe, which was longer than the car itself. He, the car, and the bronco-riding canoe had all endured a bone-shaking half hour of hard knocks before reaching the grassy clearing at Moose Lake Landing. He saw himself announcing his arrival with two short blasts of the horn, as a wake-up call for Paddy O'Malley, and then retrieving a well-shaken six pack from the trunk and heading down the trail that led to the Park Ranger's cabin.

In 1974, the living was easy for Patrick O'Malley, who was basking in the adulation of local hockey fans as he waited to report to the Detroit Red Wings training camp. Way back then, an interim grace-and-favour job as Park Ranger was just the ticket for the local hero—the most talented player to come out of Sudbury in the last decade. The living had not always been easy for O'Malley. Far from it. His father, whoever he might have been, had gone missing a few minutes after Paddy was conceived. Whether his mother was a prostitute, as was rumoured, didn't matter, since she went missing not long after he was born. Paddy had inherited nothing from his AWOL parents, except athleticism, and had received nothing from orphanages and foster homes except beatings and survival techniques. He became tough early. On the other hand, athleticism and toughness is a good skill set for the National Hockey League, and that's where Paddy's destiny was beckoning.

Manetti saw himself clattering into the Ranger's cabin and swinging the six pack onto the counter, the unofficial admission fee to the admission-free Provincial Park. Several minutes passed before O'Malley shambled from the back bedroom, yawning and rubbing sleep from his eyes. To acknowledge the beer would be to acknowledge an impropriety, so O'Malley didn't acknowledge either Manetti or the beer, except to carry the six pack into the bedroom. Manetti heard a muffled conversation and wondered whether he knew the girl.

A few more minutes passed before O'Malley reappeared. "It's the middle of the night, Rocco. Gimme a break, eh?"

"Sorry, Paddy, am I interrupting your coitus?"

"You're interruptin' my sleep, asshole." O'Malley hoisted the register from under the counter, and Manetti entered the date and time of arrival, his destination, and his expected time of departure; then he signed it. As Manetti was completing the entry, O'Malley was reading it upside down. "Wolf Island again! Out at six p.m. If you get hung up in the rapids, it's me who'll have to go fishin' for your body with the cops."

"If I drown, you can have my car for your trouble. I know it's not fancy enough for a hockey star, but you can sell it and keep the cash."

"Keep the change, you mean."

"From Sudbury to the Detroit Red Wings... We're all proud of you, Paddy. When's training camp start?"

"Next month. Where's the rich girlfriend today? *La belle Pierrette?*"

"Who says she's my girlfriend?"

"You think it's a secret? If you don't want her, I'll sure as hell take her."

"Why would I bring a girlfriend to this godforsaken place?"

"I figger it's cuz you like playin' Tarzan and Jane on Wolf Island. Like as not, she's out there right now ... hidin' in your car."

"You're hallucinating, Paddy."

"Bullshit I am. I know what's goin' on, Rocco. You sneak her into the park cuz you don't want her name in the Register, cuz her brother would kill you, and maybe her too, if he ever found out you two go campin'. Don't worry, I won't tell him."

"You've got a great imagination, Paddy."

"Imagination, my ass! Maybe I'll go down to the Landing and see for myself. Maybe I'll arrest your rich girlfriend and hold her for interrogation. I'm sure she'd like that, eh?"

"Sorry to throw cold water on your fantasies, Paddy, but I'm all alone today."

"That's a first then. Why don't you two bypass Moose Lake and fly direct into Canoe? Hell, I hear she's got her pilot's license, and her old man's sure as hell got the planes. Why's she want to shake, rattle, and roll her way here in your lousy car, and then shoot the rapids into Canoe? That's hard work, 'specially for a girl. Tell her she can fly into Canoe Lake with me anytime, day or night. 'Specially night."

"I'll tell her."

For a moment, O'Malley's face had clouded. Manetti noticed it but said nothing.

"You're playin' for Queen's I hear. None of my business what you do, but you could have made the NHL. I heard they were scoutin' you too."

"So I heard."

"So, why didn't you sign, eh?"

"I didn't get an offer. Besides, the league isn't big enough for both of us."

"Bullshit!" O'Malley's face had clouded again, and Manetti seized the moment. "You got something to tell me, Paddy."

"Probably nothin' to it."

"Tell me anyway."

"A coupl'a weeks ago, you two were down here, most likely playin' house on Wolf Island."

"Down here for the day. Fishing."

"Is that what you call it? Anyway, 'bout half an hour after you lovebirds paddled away, her brother shows up, pissed to the gills, drivin' his old man's big Mercedes. Can you imagine takin' a car like that over five miles of ruts, potholes, and washouts? Geez! Well, he busts in here like it's a police raid. Don't say, 'Hello,' 'Goodbye,' or 'Go fuck yourself.' Don't say nothin'. He just walks around the counter and starts pawin' through the register, like he owns the place, all the time rantin' like a madman, half in English, half in French."

"So, what was he saying?"

"I'm not exactly sure. I think he'd been smokin' somethin' along with the booze. Anyway, it was half in French, and I don't speak the lingo."

"Tell me the English half."

"Like I say, he was smashed; probably didn't know what he was sayin'."

"Quit stalling, Paddy! You started it. You finish it. *Capisce?*"

"Don't kill the messenger, eh?"

"I won't, but let's hear the message."

"It was mostly just swearin' and rantin', eh? He was callin' you a dago bastard, and then he said the only good dago is a dead dago, and he'd see you dead before you screwed his sister." O'Malley paused. "Look Rocco, the only reason I'm tellin' you this is 'cause he seemed serious. Crazy but serious, if you take my meanin'."

"Yes, I take your meaning. Michel Legault and I have never been buddies."

"So, tell me somethin' new. Why do you think I'm tellin' you about his little visit? Geez! I think the bugger may be crazy. I mean crazy-crazy. None of my business, I guess, but I thought you should know."

"Thanks, Paddy. I think I should know too."

"Legault's a dirty player. Always was."

"So, tell *me* something new."

"So, keep your head up and stay out of the corners."

Suddenly, a noise from somewhere jarred Manetti from the past to the present.

CHAPTER
EIGHTEEN

ONE OF THE under-rated features of urban life is that citizens can kill one another without raising eyebrows. A shooting here, a knifing there are all part of the urban roundelay, as is the odd suspicious drowning. Unlike their country cousins, or their cousins who reside in busybody county towns, city-dwellers don't care a whole hell of a lot what happens, just so long as it doesn't happen to them.

When Manetti was jarred from his memory trance, he was still alone. He waited but no police came; no one came. After fifteen minutes or so, he decided that the police weren't going to come unless he summoned them, and he decided not to summon them.

He returned to O'Malley's car, drove to Isabella Street, and parked in a lot near O'Malley's building. There he began a methodical search of the car, carefully sifting through the glove compartment, looking behind the sun visors, sliding his hands behind and under the seats, and finally checking the back deck. There were no photographs. He pocketed O'Malley's damp wallet and made a careful search of the trunk. There were no photographs there either.

After locking the car, Manetti walked half a block to the apartment building, lurking outside until he determined which key was which, and until the lobby was clear. Then he quickly entered the building and took the elevator to the fourth floor. He met no one and saw no one, although he sensed that someone was watching him.

Apartment 403 was a sloven's pad—a one-bedroom pigsty. The once-white walls were uniformly dirty and randomly stained. The once-beige broadloom was now a free-form design of grimy spills and footprints. The furniture was sparse, cheap, and gouged, with all the flat surfaces white-circled from sweating beer bottles.

There was no time to reflect on O'Malley's lousy housekeeping. As he had with the car, he began a methodical search of the apartment, carefully replacing everything so the place would look undisturbed. A professional burglar would have done the same thing, except that any self-respecting burglar would have worn gloves, and no self-respecting burglar would have wasted his talents on Apartment 403.

It took only five minutes to discover a large manila envelope containing a dozen or more incriminating photographs. It took another hour to sift through hundreds of other photographs, all of them featuring Paddy the hockey player or Paddy with his myriad girlfriends. Thorough as the search had been, Manetti worried that O'Malley might have secreted other photographs or incriminating material in the apartment, perhaps with an explanatory letter.

He opened the door a crack to check that the hallway was empty, and then quickly left the building and walked the few blocks to the intersection of Yonge and Bloor Streets. There he flagged down a taxi. At the corner of St. Clair and Avenue Road, he abandoned the taxi and walked the rest of the way home, up Avenue Road to Heath Street and then along Heath to Dunvegan Road. As he went, he unfastened the keys from O'Malley's key ring, one by one, and dropped them one by one down sewer gratings. The final drop was the key ring itself.

When he reached home, he went straight to his study and burned the photographs in the fireplace. Then he stripped O'Malley's wallet, burned what was flammable, and cut up what was plastic. Finally, he scooped the ashes into a jar, put the plastics bits into a bag, and took the dog for a walk.

Only Manetti and Oro knew where he scattered the ashes and the bits of plastic, and where he discarded the Scotch-marinated wallet.

CHAPTER
NINETEEN

ABOUT FIVE O'CLOCK on Wednesday afternoon, Alastair Drake turned up at Lunex. "I thought you were going to telephone," said Manetti, ushering him into the conference room.

"I needed a walk," replied Drake, "and the walls may have ears. Who knows?"

"Are you bearing good news or bad?"

"Mostly bad, I'm afraid."

"I've been expecting bad news," said Manetti.

"The Board has authorized me to tell you what I'm about to tell you, in strict confidence, of course."

"Understood."

"The bottom line is that Laurentian won't contest or block a Noramet bid for Lunex. Assuming a good Noramet offer, we'll tender our Lunex shares for Noramet shares, not cash. Our Directors are enthused about the potential for Mountain Lake."

"Because you enthused them."

"I guess you could say that."

"Well, they're right to be enthused, and so are you. You said *mostly* bad news. Is there some good news?"

"Hypothetical good news at best... *Long-shot* good news at best. If for any reason Noramet's takeover bid doesn't materialize, Laurentian's Board would welcome a friendly Laurentian/Lunex merger. We'd be pleased to take Lunex into protective custody as a Laurentian subsidiary, and you as my successor I should add."

"I'm obviously disappointed Laurentian doesn't want us enough to duke it out with Noramet for the big prize."

"I know you're disappointed, Rocco. So am I. But I'm here to report, not to negotiate."

Manetti nodded. "If I were on the Laurentian Board, I'd probably have come to the same decision. Unfortunately for Lunex, Noramet's bid isn't likely to fall by the wayside."

"Unfortunately for both Laurentian and Lunex, it looks that way. On the other hand, *it ain't over 'til it's over...*"

"I said the same thing to Warren," interrupted Manetti, "but it was just a blandishment. Like ... *Where there's life there's hope.* Spare me the consolatory platitudes, Alastair." Manetti shook his head in frustration. "I can see, hear, and smell Macdonald promoting the Noramet bid. Sorry. I know it's none of my damn business who said what to whom."

"You're right, it isn't. However, since you raise the point, I can tell you that Ross didn't open his mouth during the meeting. He neither supported nor opposed my recommendations."

"I thought Macdonald would be unalterably opposed to the white-knight option."

"He is, but he's also street smart. I guess he figured that open disagreement with my recommendations wouldn't advance his career, so he shut the hell up and sat on the fence. That said, I understand he did some behind-the-scenes lobbying before the meeting. That's another matter which needn't burden you." He paused. "In any event, whether or not he lobbied a few of our Directors, the Board would have come to the same decision, and as you just pointed out, perhaps it's the right decision for Laurentian."

"Well, thanks for going to bat for Lunex."

"I went to bat for Laurentian, and I'm as disappointed as you are."

"My group had a final council-of-war this morning. We hashed it out and decided that, if Laurentian went the way it has, we'd tender to Noramet for cash—there'll be lots of it—and start another company. We don't want any Noramet shares stinking up our portfolio."

"Actually, this black cloud has two silver linings for you," said Drake. "You'll make a fortune tendering your shares to Noramet, and since Laurentian won't be acquiring Lunex, you won't be sent into servitude as my successor. Forgive my saying so, Rocco, but you look terrible. Don't let this takeover business affect your health."

"I'm okay. Thanks for your concern, but I'm okay. I had a rough night, that's all."

CHAPTER
TWENTY

UNTIL THE UNLISTED telephone rang, Richard Fennell and Susan Blair had been enjoying a candlelight dinner at the Noramet apartment. Fennell threw his napkin to the table and strode impatiently into the study, ready to excoriate the Noramet officer who was foolhardy enough to interrupt his dalliance.

"Hello!"

"Dick! Ross Macdonald here. Sorry to bother you at home."

Fennell grimaced. "Quite okay, Ross, quite okay, but how did you get this number?"

"From Bill Graydon. He asked me to give you a call. Is this a good time?"

"Fine, Ross, fine. How did your meeting go?"

"Good news! Drake made an aggressive pitch for the white-knight option, but at the risk of being immodest, my counter arguments carried the day. The bottom line is that Laurentian won't oppose a Noramet bid."

"Excellent work, Ross! I knew you'd deliver the goods. Anything else I should know?"

"Yes, the Board likes Mountain Lake, so assuming Noramet goes forward with a takeover bid, they'll be looking to exchange our Lunex shares for Noramet shares rather than cash."

"That's no problem. We'll structure a cash or share offer. We might even be magnanimous and offer Laurentian a seat on Noramet's Board. Maybe you'll be our new Director."

"Not while Drake's still around, that's for sure. Of course, Laurentian support for a Noramet bid will depend on an attractive bid. I guess that goes without saying."

"No worries on that score; we won't lowball Lunex. Anything else?"

"If the Noramet bid doesn't go forward for any reason, the Laurentian Board would support a friendly Laurentian/Lunex merger, but as I said, it won't contest a Noramet bid."

"Very wise of the Laurentian Board. I can assure you that Noramet's going to proceed with its bid, unless Lunex spares us the time and trouble by selling us Mountain Lake outright."

"My guess is you'll have to go the takeover route."

"That's my guess too. Anything else?"

"Yes, Drake was expressly authorized to inform Manetti of the Board's decision, but no one at Laurentian would approve of my briefing Noramet. I guess this goes without saying too."

"Ross, you can rely on my absolute discretion. I'll be in Toronto tomorrow afternoon—a showdown meeting with Manetti—so your call is timely. Thanks again for your good work."

CHAPTER
TWENTY-ONE

FOLLOWING HIS MEETING with Drake, Manetti drove straight home, dog-tired, dejected, and worried. He was dejected about losing Lunex and worried about O'Malley. He had lain awake most of Tuesday night, wondering when and where O'Malley's body would wash up, wondering when the police would come knocking on his door. He was also worried that he felt no guilt, and he wondered whether psychopathic killers rationalize and excuse their crimes as he was doing, on the grounds that they hadn't intended to kill their victims. Was he, in fact, a psychopathic killer? He couldn't deny that he'd been lethally sober, whilst O'Malley had been helplessly drunk. Had he really intended to save O'Malley? Would he really have dived into the harbour if O'Malley had surfaced? He wondered and he worried.

Manetti knew that he needed sleep to clear his head. He'd need a clear head if and when the police came calling, and he'd also need a damn good criminal lawyer. He dropped his briefcase in the front hall and went straight to the kitchen for a beer. Oro didn't come waddling and wagging to meet him, which meant he'd been banished. Maria cleaned house on Wednesdays and routinely banished the overly affectionate dog to the back garden.

There was a casserole in the microwave and a note giving precise, albeit misspelled, instructions about operating the machine. When it came to kitchen matters, both Pierrette and Maria thought of him as a retarded schoolboy. He pressed the numbers in accordance with the instructions, which concluded by saying that "in exakly 10 minutes the dinger will ding." There was a postscript—Maria's signature joke: "Your dog is in the doghouse."

Manetti turned on an all-news radio station, both hoping and fearing that O'Malley's body had been recovered. When the news items began repeating themselves, he switched off the radio, picked up the *Globe and Mail*, and crossed the hall to his study. As he sank wearily into his reading chair, the beer glass fell from his hand and shattered, all unnoticed, as he took in a scene of pure horror. Across the room sat Oro, staring back at him from the desk chair, like a human dog escaped from a Coolidge painting, sitting upright in the chair, a forepaw draped casually over each arm. A framed wedding photograph of Pierrette and Rocco had been torn from the wall, propped on the seat of the chair, and jammed against the dog's belly, holding the animal upright as if he were displaying the picture.

Manetti bolted across the room to confirm what he knew. Oro was dead. On the desk, there was a scrawled note: *"First the dog – then you, partner – then Pierrette. I'll have a ball doing Pierrette."*

There was a moment of disbelief as he stared at the grotesquerie before him. Then came howls of grief, as he carried his old pet to the kitchen and laid him in his bed by the stove. Then came fear and rage. He was shaking uncontrollably as he took another beer from the refrigerator and returned to the study, oblivious to the broken glass that crunched underfoot, oblivious to the beer-soaked rug and the brewery fumes which filled the room. O'Malley was alive. O'Malley was alive and stalking Pierrette and him. O'Malley was alive and had strangled Oro. O'Malley was a madman.

A few minutes earlier, Manetti had been worrying about his own sanity. Now he prayed that he was indeed insane, so that he could take on O'Malley without the constraints of sanity—madman to madman. He was trapped and alone, and he knew it. He and

O'Malley would stalk each other until one of them killed the other, and he knew that too. The police wouldn't be coming for him, but O'Malley would.

As he fully comprehended the fact that he was destined to kill or be killed, Manetti became eerily calm and collected. He located O'Malley's point of entry: the jimmied kitchen door, which Maria had left locked but not dead-bolted. Then he bolted that door. Next, he secured the other doors and windows and activated the security system. That done, he went to bed, and to his surprise, slept soundly.

CHAPTER
TWENTY-TWO

MANETTI WOKE EARLY. It was still dark when he buried Oro in the back garden. It was not yet six-thirty when he drove to a nearby telephone booth and called O'Malley.

"What?" came a half-asleep and surly voice.

"You killed Oro."

There was loud coughing and throat clearing as O'Malley's body and mind got into gear and into sync. "*Oro*... Was that his name? Sounds like a good wop name for a wop dog, eh?" O'Malley was wide awake now. "He came runnin' up to be patted, so I strangled him. I was thinkin' of drownin' him in that fancy swimmin' pool of yours. Kind of tit for tat, since you tried to drown me, but it was easier just to strangle him. I never did like dogs. It's payback time, wop-boy. You're next!"

"No, O'Malley, you're next. Tuesday was an accident, but I couldn't care less whether you believe me. It's too late now."

"Sure, it was an accident. First, you *accidentally* spiked my booze. Then you *accidentally* stole my money. Then you *accidentally* knocked me into the lake. Then you *accidentally* stole my car and *accidentally* broke into my apartment. Lucky for me, I have extra keys. Unlucky for you, you didn't get all the pichers."

"By this time tomorrow, you'll be dead, O'Malley, and this time it won't be an accident."

"The only accident Tuesday night was me washin' up under the pier and bein' able to hang on to one of them slimy logs 'til I heard you steal my car and bugger off. You see, wop-boy, I've got nine lives, like a cat. Not like your dog, and not like you ... and not like that pretty wife of yours."

"I'm putting out a contract on you, O'Malley, so by this time tomorrow, you'll have disappeared without a trace. They'll never find your body ... not that anyone will look very hard."

"Big talk from a bullshit wop."

"In some ways, I'd enjoy killing you myself, but why soil my hands on a piece of trash? I'll leave you to the professionals, you son of a whore."

"Come over here and say that to my face."

"I'll leave you to the professionals, brothel boy. Drink up today, because tomorrow you're gone, and since you kill little dogs, I'll tell the boys to work you over before they kill you."

"You're a coward, Manetti. Too much of a coward to fight your own battles, you yella-bellied wop."

"I'm not afraid to fight you, O'Malley, but it'll have to be tonight, because you'll be dead tomorrow."

"Call off your dogs, and I'll fight you tonight. Call off your dogs, unless you're a coward."

"Okay, tonight it is! Just you and me."

"Name the place."

"You know where I live, brothel-boy."

O'Malley didn't reply. There was a long silence and then the dial tone.

Manetti knew where the fight would take place. Advantage to him. He didn't know how or when it would begin. Advantage to O'Malley. He did know that there would be no rules of engagement, and that it would be a fight to the finish.

Just past nine o'clock, Manetti telephoned Ann Stevenson to say he'd be working from home all morning.

"That's a first," responded Stevenson, but her instincts told her to say no more. "You have an appointment with Richard Fennell at three o'clock."

"Yes, I remember. I'll be in around noon, so hold my calls."

That done, he re-checked all doors and windows and confirmed that the security system was on alarm. He doubted that O'Malley would come for him during daylight hours, but then again. it had been a daylight invasion yesterday.

Manetti spent the next hour handwriting an unflinching account of Legault's death and O'Malley's blackmail, following which he photocopied the manuscript, enclosed the photostat in an envelope addressed to Warren Ransom, and enclosed the original in an envelope addressed to Pierrette. To Ransom's envelope, he added detailed instructions about actions to be taken to protect Pierrette. To Pierrette's envelope, he added a letter begging forgiveness, warning that her life was in imminent danger and imploring her to co-operate with Warren Ransom in devising security measures to safeguard her life. Then he put both envelopes in his wall safe and telephoned Ransom at the Mountain Lake camp.

"Warren, you'll be driving in from Oakville tomorrow morning, right?"

"Right."

"Good! Can you do me a favour? I've decided to drive up to the cottage early tomorrow morning, so can you detour by the house on your way into the office and pick up a couple of envelopes."

"No problem! I should be there about eight."

"Look, if you don't get an answer, use the spare key to the front door. You know where we leave it. The files will be on top of my desk. It's very important, Warren. In fact, it's vital ... so don't leave without getting them."

"No problem. Rocco, are you okay?"

"Never better. Why?"

"You sound strange."

"Stranger than usual?"

"I think so ... and the request sounds rather strange too. Anyway, I'll see you tomorrow morning, failing which I'll break and enter."

"Don't break anything, just enter ... and thanks."

He hung up, surprised and grateful that his mind was clear and concentrated. He'd need a clear and concentrated mind when O'Malley did show up. If the madman didn't come hunting him tonight, he'd have to go hunting the madman tomorrow. He and O'Malley were both cornered.

CHAPTER
TWENTY-THREE

IT WAS WELL after four o'clock when Fennell arrived for his three o'clock appointment. Manetti didn't extend the courtesy of receiving him in the lobby. Instead, he stayed put in his office and let Ann Stevenson fetch Caesar.

The two men shook hands, more like two boxers touching gloves before a fight, neither deigning to acknowledge Fennell's impunctuality. When Manetti gestured to a chair, Fennell moved to the window instead and remained standing. "A great view, Rocco, I envy you. In Manhattan, every building is hemmed in … a slice of vista here, a patch of sky there, claustrophobia everywhere. Toronto hasn't lost its space." Having thus asserted his independence, Fennell sat down. "Isn't Warren Ransom going to join us?"

"He declined my invitation."

Fennell shrugged dismissively. "It's been a long time, Rocco, a long time since you and I were colleagues at Noramet."

"Ah yes, *the good old days,*" responded Manetti sarcastically.

"Still bitter after all these years! You know, Rocco, I had nothing to do with that Pericatu shuffle; nothing whatsoever."

"I'm not bitter at all. Pericatu was my get-out-of-jail card."

Fennell shrugged again. "I must say I value your frankness more than your courtesy."

"I have neither time nor talent for bullshit, so let's get down to business."

"Okay, have it your way. I'm here to give you one last chance before we proceed with our takeover bid. As you well know, we don't want Lunex, we want Mountain Lake, so you can save us a lot of trouble and yourself a lot of grief by selling us that one asset. We're ready, willing, and able to pay top dollar for your Mountain Lake properties. *Top dollar.* However, unless Bill Graydon got it wrong, you're dead set against selling Mountain Lake to Noramet or anyone else."

"Especially Noramet! Graydon got it right, so why don't you take *no* for an answer and bugger off."

"As one of our distinguished alumni, you should remember that I never take no for an answer, and I've never been known to *bugger off* from a good fight. If I took no for an answer, Noramet wouldn't be the world's premier gold producer. We know what we want, and we get what we want. One way or the other. If I may say so, Rocco, you look stressed out. Are you afraid of a good fight?"

"No, not the one you have in mind anyway. Too bad the *premier gold producer* can't make its own discoveries anymore. Mountain Lake is our discovery, not Noramet's."

"We do less field exploration than once we did, because it's more cost-effective to buy orebodies that fit our portfolio."

"A jackal feeding off the lion's kill."

"The jackal feeds last. Noramet feeds first. Don't flatter yourself by calling Lunex a lion or Noramet a jackal. If Lunex is a lion, then Noramet is a much bigger and hungrier lion. Leave off the jungle metaphors. Leave off the taunts. Face facts."

"You talk about paying *top-dollar* for Mountain Lake, but just how can you or anyone else put a price on it now? These are early days."

"*Top-dollar* is paying for the sizzle as well as the steak, which means we'll be overpaying. *Top-dollar* is whatever it takes to discourage competing bids, which means we'll be overpaying, since Noramet will be negotiating against itself. If you prefer, *top-dollar* is whatever Mountain Lake will fetch at auction. So put Mountain Lake on the auction block, and Noramet will acquire it that way ... and at a lower price."

"Bullshit! You're trying to scoop Mountain Lake before the Lunex shareholders know what they've got."

"Don't forget that Noramet is a Lunex shareholder too, and Noramet commends you on your excellent timely disclosure. You've been telling all your shareholders what they've got; there's a fresh media release every other day. If there's more to tell, there'll be more media releases. If you force us into a takeover bid for Lunex, it will be up to the Lunex shareholders to evaluate our offer, and they'll have plenty of professional advice on what constitutes fair value."

"Our shareholders don't yet know what they've got, because we don't yet know what they've got."

"This is the real world, Rocco, so face facts. Noramet will get Mountain Lake one way or the other, and the win/win way is a negotiated agreement. If you embrace the win/win way, you make a fortune and keep Lunex. The other way you make a fortune but lose Lunex. Either way you lose Mountain Lake. As a matter of fact, Thorne Sullivan calculates that it would be more cost-effective for Noramet to go the takeover route, given your undervalued share price, so we're doing you a *favour* by offering to buy Mountain Lake."

"Lunex may not be as vulnerable as you think we are."

"No? As we see it, your one hope is Laurentian, but according to our intelligence, Laurentian isn't going to be your white knight."

"Perhaps you're getting bad intelligence."

Fennell shrugged. "Look, let's quit sparring. I take it you're refusing our offer."

"I haven't seen your offer."

"If we have agreement in principle, Noramet will submit a formal offer soon enough, but if you've hung a *Not-for-Sale* sign on Mountain Lake, then we're not going to spin our wheels."

"I can only speak for myself," replied Manetti. "I can't speak for the Lunex Board. If I were to recommend to my Board that we sell Mountain Lake, I'd call it a recommendation *in perversion of principle*. However, submit your offer to me, and I'll submit it to the Lunex Board."

"You're being disingenuous, Rocco. You're the Chairman and CEO of Lunex. You're the directing mind of Lunex, so if you don't recommend it, the Board won't approve it."

Manetti smiled sardonically. "Who knows? Maybe they'll approve it over my dead body."

"Not according to our intelligence," said Fennell.

"It's an ugly game you're playing, Fennell."

"Golf and tennis are the only games I play. Everything else is strictly business."

"You play games all right. Ugly games. The mining industry has scars to prove that you regard it as a game for the aggrandizement of Richard Fennell. Are your Directors as ruthless as you? Or do you mislead them?"

"*Ruthless* is a loser's word. A loser's lament. If you weren't bare-ass to the wind, you wouldn't be feeding me that slop. Around Noramet, I propose and I dispose. It's as simple as that. Somewhere between proposal and disposal, I get Board approval."

"So, you have a Board of trained seals."

"They're not trained seals, but they don't second guess me too often. Why? Because I've got a great track record, and because Noramet needs me more than I need Noramet. The first time they reject a serious proposal from me is the last time they'll see me, and they know it."

"I guess that's my cue to applaud. You've said what you came to say, and you've made your position crystal clear."

"I've never believed in pussy-footing. Pussy-footing sends mixed messages and suggests a lack of resolve."

"I understand your message and your resolve. I'll sleep on it over the weekend and give you my answer on Tuesday."

"*Tuesday?* What's wrong with right now? You've had lots of time to sleep on it, Rocco, lots of time. Now's the time to wake up before you lose your company."

"Thanks for the advice. Believe it or not, I have more pressing matters on my plate right now. I'll give you our answer on Tuesday."

"What makes you think I'll wait?"

"Do what you have to do."

Fennell paused for a long moment. "Okay, Rocco, I'll give you until Tuesday morning to come to your senses. As it happens, I have meetings in Toronto on Tuesday, and since I don't trust telephones, I'll drop by in the morning, say ten o'clock. I won't be looking for more surly exchanges. I'll be looking for a simple *yes* or *no*, agreement in principle or not."

"Ten o'clock's fine. I assume ten o'clock means any time before noon." He rang for his secretary. "Ann will see you out."

"It's decision time, Rocco, so don't try to waltz me around."

"Believe me, Richard Fennell the third, you're the very last person I'd want to dance with."

"You lend new meaning to the term *hostile takeover*," responded Fennell. "If you'll permit some personal advice, sincere personal advice, get some rest on the weekend. As I said, you look and sound stressed out."

"I guarantee that you'll know my position on Tuesday. Maybe sooner," replied Manetti. "Who knows how the universe is about to unfold?"

CHAPTER
TWENTY-FOUR

AFTER FENNELL LEFT, Manetti worked for a couple of hours and then went to the National Club for a solitary dinner. How should he prepare for the upcoming showdown? He had no idea. As he ate, he realized with horror that he might not live to eat again. Even odds at best.

It was getting dark when he pulled into his driveway. He sat in the car for a few minutes to satisfy himself that O'Malley wasn't lurking in the shadows. Then he cautiously circled the house to satisfy himself that O'Malley hadn't broken into the place already. Then he went inside.

Assuming O'Malley was going to come for him tonight, Manetti would have to leave the house accessible, but not obviously accessible. To that end, he deactivated the security system and unbolted the kitchen door. He didn't unlock the kitchen door, since O'Malley knew well enough how to jimmy that lock.

With the downstairs in darkness and vulnerable to break-in, Manetti started upstairs. Responding to an afterthought, he returned to the living room and picked up a poker from the fireplace set. Then he went upstairs.

His home turf advantage was starting to seem less of an advantage and more of a trap. If and when O'Malley came for him, Manetti would be trapped there, trying to kill or escape a psychopathic killer.

O'Malley had been inside the house yesterday and knew the layout, at least the downstairs layout. Perhaps O'Malley had prowled the place yesterday and knew the upstairs layout as well.

Whether or not he was trapped, there was no turning back now. Manetti didn't know what to do if O'Malley did come after him, and didn't know what to do if he didn't come, but he did know he had to stay calm and avoid recklessness. All he could do was wait and stay calm.

He went to the master bedroom and switched on a bedside lamp and the radio. With soft music playing in the background, he left the room, half closing the door behind him. Then he moved across the hall to the den, settled himself in an easy chair, and began his long vigil. As he sat in the dark, he was fighting panic, sensing that death was lurking nearby but not knowing whether the Grim Reaper was stalking him or O'Malley. One of them would be the killer, one the victim … or maybe there'd be two victims.

Manetti sat in the dark for the better part of two hours, listening intently. The first noise he heard sounded like a shoe scraping on marble. Then there was silence. The noise had been faint, and Manetti thought it might have been the bedroom radio. He had almost convinced himself that the noise had come from the bedroom when he heard it again. This time it was distinct and came from downstairs.

O'Malley was in the house and had come for him. Waiting for the battle to begin had been unnerving, but Manetti had not lost his self control. He eased himself out of the chair and moved stealthily across the room in stocking feet, pressing himself against the den wall. Looking sideways, he had an unobstructed view down the upstairs hallway, and through the banister railings, he had a partial view of the top few steps of the staircase.

There were no further noises, which meant that O'Malley was either standing still on the marble floor of the downstairs foyer or moving noiselessly on broadloom. If he was on broadloom, he was either prowling the downstairs rooms or cautiously mounting the carpeted stairway. Several minutes passed before a giant shadow appeared on the stairwell wall, head and shoulders silhouetted by the narrow beam of light that escaped from the bedroom, streamed across the hallway, and through the banister railings. Then O'Malley himself came into view, as he slowly and warily ascended the last few stairs and reached the upstairs hallway, staring suspiciously at the half-closed door to the bedroom, sensing a trap. He stood there in suspended animation, a statue wielding a large hunting knife, obviously uncertain about moving further, and obviously trying to glean some sense of Manetti's whereabouts.

After several minutes, O'Malley began to move cautiously down the hall. When he neared the pathway of light, he stopped again, listening intently, and then moved quickly past the door to the end of the hallway. Now he was outside the den, standing directly opposite Manetti, standing on the opposite side of the same wall. Although Manetti could no longer see him, he could hear O'Malley's heavy breathing and wondered why O'Malley couldn't hear Manetti's pounding heart.

Suddenly, steely calm abandoned Manetti and reckless fury took charge. Roaring like a madman, he leaped into the hallway and swung the poker with all his strength. O'Malley whirled and slashed the air as the poker caught him on the chest and drove him against the banister. The knife slashed again, and Manetti, dodging the blade, lost his balance and fell. As O'Malley raised the knife to strike home, Manetti rolled to his knees, grabbed O'Malley's ankles, and tipped him backwards over the banister.

O'Malley was briefly in free fall, still clutching the knife. He bounced once off the downstairs banister before hitting the marble foyer. There was a sharp crack—a skull-splitting crack.

Manetti moved to the top of the staircase and looked down at the crumpled body. Then he slowly descended the stairs, praying that O'Malley was dead, knowing that he possessed neither the courage nor the cowardice to finish him off if he wasn't.

CHAPTER
TWENTY-FIVE

DRAKE WAS WATCHING the eleven o'clock news when Seagram telephoned to report that Drake's office had been bugged and that a receiver had been located in Macdonald's office. "I guess that's what you suspected," said Seagram.

"That's what I feared," replied Drake.

"Macdonald signed in Friday evening but didn't sign anyone else in. No surprise there. Shall I tell them to remove the mic's?"

"No, not tonight. Not right away. What if you just transferred the receiver to my office?"

"You want to bug yourself?"

"Something like that. I guess."

"Do you want them to take fingerprints from the receiver?"

"Yes. I'm afraid things could turn nasty."

"I know where you'd like to shove this receiver, but I'll leave it on your desk, if that's what you want."

"Maybe *in* my desk would be better. Do you have a key?"

"I have keys to every lock in the place."

"You're a dangerous fellow. How does the receiver work?"

"By tape. Nobody has audited the tape."

"Except Macdonald. I'll listen to it in the morning, although I know what's on it."

"There are a bunch more cassettes in the drawer, although they look unused. We can check them out in the morning."

"I'm sorry to drag you into this mess, Jack ... but thanks."

"No problem. I'm sorry there's villainy afoot, but I'm glad the villain turned out to be Macdonald. If it's of any interest to you, our security people are impressed with the work. Whoever bugged your office is a real pro."

"I guess I should be flattered. To be bugged by an amateur would be insulting, as Oscar Wilde might have said."

CHAPTER
TWENTY-SIX

MANETTI'S PRAYERS WERE answered. O'Malley was dead. He sat on the bottom step, shaking uncontrollably, wondering absently why there was no blood on the floor. He sat there in shock, staring at the corpse as he re-lived in detail the events that now, more than four decades later, had led to O'Malley's death.

In 1974, Rocco Manetti had but two ambitions, the first to win Pierrette Legault for his bride, and the second to be gold medallist in his year. He was confident that he would realize his second ambition, but was in despair about the first. He recognized full well the bleak facts of life confronting Pierrette and him. She would have to be strong, but she was still too young to be strong, still too dependent on her family and family approval. Things looked hopeless.

His mind was in turmoil as he launched the canoe and paddled away from Moose Lake Landing. Looked at from the perspective of the Legault family, he was an unsuitable match for Pierrette—of that, he was painfully aware. For one thing—the main thing—he was not Quebecois; for another, he was poor. He was proud of his family and his heritage, but he knew full well that the son of an Italian immigrant would not be embraced by the almighty Legaults.

Even if his Florentine uncles were merchant princes, Rocco Manetti would be regarded by the Legault clan as an unsuitable match for Pierrette. He was not Quebecois.

There was a smart breeze from the northwest, which made for easy paddling. For the most part, he just steered the canoe and let the current carry him down-lake towards the narrows. If the wind held steady, there'd be stiff paddling on the return trip.

Pierrette's family didn't know about their engagement. He was sure she wouldn't tell them, but her brother certainly knew they'd been seeing each other and had probably told their parents. The cat was out of the bag, which surely must explain Pierrette's unscheduled visit to Quebec City. Her parents had obviously sent her out of harm's way while they pondered the problem; and now O'Malley's warning confirmed his fears that Michel Legault would do everything in his power to come between Pierrette and him.

Now the canoe was approaching the white water where Moose Lake funnels into Canoe Lake. There were two signs there, one marking the portage between the two lakes and the other prohibiting boaters from shooting the rapids. On only four occasions had Manetti declined the challenge of the rapids: the four occasions on which Pierrette had been with him. Today, he swung into the strong current without hesitation, and for the next few minutes, forgot about Pierrette as he concentrated on saving his skin. He made it through in one piece, although there had been two close calls and a scraped gunnel to prove it. There was arduous paddling now as he headed upwind for Wolf Island. He beached the canoe there and unloaded a bedroll and a geology text. He'd come to study.

Manetti had the immigrant's drive to succeed, the kid from nowhere pitting his brains and ambition against an indifferent world—a world teeming with brainy and ambitious kids, some from somewhere, some from nowhere, some with connections, and some without. He lived with the stark reality that he was at Queen's on scholarships, which were conditional upon unfaltering academic achievement. No scholarships, no Queen's. He would be the only student in his class to read and master his second-year texts before his sophomore year began.

A couple of hundred feet along the beach stood a half-abandoned log cabin, someone's erstwhile cottage that the Ontario Government had expropriated when the provincial park was established. The Park Authority had never bothered to knock it down, nor had they bothered to maintain it. However, that sturdy little cabin refused to collapse from neglect, and stood year after year as a foul-weather shelter for fishermen and as a permanent residence for successive generations of mice. Although it was a primitive structure, it had a solid roof (albeit mossy), unbroken windows (albeit filthy), a wood stove (albeit rusty), and a functioning door (albeit creaky). It also had a stout heart. Manetti had sheltered there in the past, but there would be no need to disturb the mice on such a fine day.

He settled himself against a large pine tree and set to work. The thick cushion of needles was a comfortable seat and the round bedroll made a comfortable backrest. Ordinarily, Manetti's disciplined mind would have ripped into the text, but today he was preoccupied with O'Malley's account of Legault's tirade. Today, his concentration abandoned him altogether. His distracted mind wandered and floated, and then surrendered to a fitful and demon-filled sleep.

He awoke with a start, momentarily disoriented and then wide awake, staring up at a real demon who was towering over him, legs astride, brandishing a baseball bat.

"Stay away from Pierrette, you dago bastard, or you'll be one dead dago bastard!"

Manetti got to his feet, cautiously, as one confronting a wild animal. "Where the hell did you come from?"

"I've been waiting for you in that shit-hole of a cabin."

"Where's your canoe?"

"Only Indians use canoes. Indians and poor-boy dago bastards. Not hard to track a dago bastard from the air though. Not hard at all. It's like tracking a rabid skunk."

Ignoring the taunts, Manetti picked up the fallen textbook. "This cost me fifty bucks," he complained, brushing it clean of sand and pine needles. It was clear from Legault's flushed face that he'd been drinking, and it was abundantly clear that he was pumping himself up for a fight. Manetti checked his own temper and played for time. "You've brought the bat, so where's the ball?"

"Your head's the ball, dago bastard." Legault made a feinting lunge, but Manetti stood his ground. "The Legaults don't want dago blood in the family, so stay away from my sister. A long way away." He made another feinting lunge, and Manetti noted that he lurched slightly.

"Pierrette's over eighteen. She doesn't belong to you or anyone else."

"She's a Legault, and she belongs to the Legaults, dago boy. She'll never belong to you."

Manetti managed to keep his self-control. "Let me get this straight. You tell Pierrette whom she may and may not date?"

"No, dago boy, just who she can't date. She's my twin sister, so I've got to protect her honour … and the family's honour."

It was clear to Manetti that the fight was unavoidable and that his best chance would be to trigger it himself, even though the odds were stacked against him. Legault was head and shoulders taller than Manetti and was brandishing a club. "You should have been born a couple of hundred years ago, Legault. You could have run your sister's life back then."

"I run it now, dago boy, so you'll never sleep with her."

Manetti took a deep breath. "I already have, froggie-face. Didn't she tell you?" He dove to the ground, as Legault swung the bat and then rolled back to his feet and hurled the textbook like a discus, a fluke shot that caught Legault full in the throat and felled him.

Not realizing that the fight was over, Manetti snatched up the fallen bat. Then the truth struck home, and he let it fall to the ground. He knelt by the limp body and felt for a pulse. There was none. Commingled emotions—horror, fear, guilt, remorse, and elation—swept over Manetti as he stared down at the lifeless body and comprehended the stark truth. He had killed a man. He had killed Pierrette's twin brother. He had killed his tormenter.

Manetti's state of shock was energizing rather than paralyzing. He retrieved a rusty shovel from a cob-webbed corner of the cabin, and robot-like, marched off through the bush until he came upon a small clearing. To rid himself of Michel Legault forever—forever and forever—the deepest pit would be too shallow. He tried to dig deep. He tried his damndest to dig deep, but he hit bedrock three feet down.

Manetti marched back to the corpse, grabbed it under the arms, and began hauling Legault towards his final resting place. This undertaker wasn't gliding a coffin-trolley down a church aisle, he was manhandling two hundred pounds of dead meat through dense bush. It was slow progress, hauling the body backwards foot by foot, heaving it over rocks and fallen trees. It was back-breaking work, and neither the sore-loser corpse nor the rough terrain was cooperating. Only shock and adrenalin made the grisly task possible.

After twenty minutes of tough schlepping, Manetti and Legault reached the pit, whereupon Manetti rolled him unceremoniously into the hole. He shovelled the dirt back, tramped it down, shovelled some more to even the ground, and then raked the site with leafy branches until the outline of the grave was blurred. Next, he rolled several boulders onto the grave, not from respect for the deceased but for fear that animals might unearth the body. He finished the job by strewing brush all about the gravesite.

It was a mean and shallow grave, well suited to a mean and shallow person.

Although Manetti was exhausted, there was still work to do. He staggered along the trail, which twists through the bush from one side of the island to the other, this time using the shovel to steady himself. There was the float plane, carefully beached and waiting for its pilot—the float plane Indians and dago bastards couldn't afford. He untied the plane, pushed it into the lake, and waited several minutes until it was caught in the current and floating free. Then he erased the pontoon marks from the sand by raking the beach with a leafy branch.

His work done, he sat on a log and rested for a while, watching the plane as it drifted smartly down-lake towards the rapids. Before long, it would pass the rapids and finally drift into the marshes at the foot of the lake. When he got his second wind, he returned to the south side of the island, tossed the baseball bat into the lake, tossed the shovel into the cabin, threw his bedroll and textbook into the canoe, and pushed off ... never to return.

Although it was easy downwind paddling towards the rapids, Manetti paddled furiously. He didn't look up until he reached the portage, by which time the float plane was a distant speck on the horizon. He gazed back at Wolf Island and crossed himself, and as he did so, he knew that Pierrette was suddenly with him there, grieving but not reproaching him. He sat with her a quarter of an hour or more, and then she was suddenly gone.

Manetti stripped off and went swimming, scrubbing himself clean of sweat and grime and trying to scrub away the deed. He had yet to learn that he would live with the ghost of Michel Legault for the rest of his life. He had yet to discover that he would never be able to scrub away the deed.

He portaged the canoe into Moose Lake, where he started the tough windward paddle. It was approaching two o'clock when he reached the landing and strapped the canoe to the roof racks. Fishermen were supposed to check out with the Park Ranger when they left, but he didn't trust himself to carry it off. O'Malley was observant and sly, much smarter than he appeared. Whether or not he asked, he would wonder why Manetti was leaving early and why he was looking so grubby. You don't get grave grime on your shirt from fishing. O'Malley would also wonder why Manetti was looking so nervous, and Manetti was indeed nervous, shaking uncontrollably from physical and nervous exhaustion. He decided to bypass the checkout and just clear out.

When he reached the highway, Manetti pulled into a gas station and telephoned. "I forgot to check out, Paddy, but I am out, so you can cross me off."

"I know you're out. I saw you go. Don't forget what I told you this mornin', eh? Keep your head up and stay out of the corners."

"Thanks, I won't forget."

As reported in the newspapers, a party of gold-plated fishermen had flown into Canoe Lake on Sunday morning. As they landed, the pilot spotted the Legault Industries' plane floating free at the swampy end of the lake. Having deposited four fishermen and two canoes on Wolf Island, he taxied down-lake to the abandoned plane, which was chafing gently against sand-mired logs. He secured it, shouted a few times for the pilot, and then radioed the Ontario Provincial Police, who were indeed looking for the missing plane, as well as the missing Legault scion.

The search was exhaustive, but Michel Legault's body was never found, at least by the authorities. Of the six parties that had logged in with the Park Ranger on the weekend, five had not ventured beyond Moose Lake. Rocco Manetti had crossed into Canoe Lake, and told the police he had fished off Wolf Island for a couple of hours but hadn't seen Legault or the float plane. Several native trappers from the adjacent Reserve had seen a float plane land on Saturday morning but hadn't been curious about it, since the lake was often visited by flying fishermen.

The police investigation concluded that Legault was presumed drowned, although the investigators and the family were troubled and made suspicious by the fact that his body never surfaced. The native trappers wondered about the same thing.

Distraught as she was, Pierrette chose Michel's funeral as the time to let her grieving family know that she had chosen Rocco Manetti. Irony of ironies, she did so by requesting Manetti to sit with her and the Legault family at the funeral mass, and by insisting that he do so when he tried to decline.

After the service, he drove with her in one of the funeral limousines, but when it swept up to the Legault mansion, he indicated with a slight shake of the head that he wouldn't go inside. She embraced him there. "I love him, and I love you, but he hated you and would have kept us apart. He would have harmed you; I know that. I prayed to the Blessed Virgin." She stared at him through tear-filled eyes. "It's not your fault, Rocco. It's God's answer. It's God's will."

He had always wondered but never dared ask what she meant by that absolution. "It's not your fault, Rocco." He had always wondered what mystical knowledge she possessed, but he never dared ask. She had been with him at the portage on that fateful day, that he knew for certain. Her presence there had been real, incorporeal but nonetheless real. Did she know—consciously know—that she'd been there, and what had happened to Michel? He never dared ask.

After a few minutes, his memory trance stopped, as did his shaking, and he went into action. As if it were pre-planned, he went down to the basement in search of the steamer trunk that had gone with him to Queen's.

With the help of a two-wheeled dolly, he bumped the heavy trunk upstairs and positioned it beside the body. Then he hoisted, pulled, bent, and stuffed O'Malley into his impromptu coffin. As an afterthought, Manetti tossed in the hunting knife. At least O'Malley didn't go unarmed into the afterlife.

That done, he rested for a few minutes before tipping the trunk onto the dolly, wheeling it to the garage, and wrestling it into the back of his Lexus SUV.

His grisly work done, Manetti took a long shower, followed by two sleeping pills. Before he surrendered to sleep, he set the alarm for six o'clock.

CHAPTER
TWENTY-SEVEN

AT SIX O'CLOCK, Manetti was jolted awake by the alarm. As he lay in bed, he felt strangely elated, notwithstanding the homicidal horrors of last night, or perhaps, because of them. He mourned Oro but had avenged his pet, and vengeance brought with it a sense of closure. After breakfast, he phoned Ransom. "Warren, there's nothing to pick up here. I'll take the files with me and call you from the cottage."

"You sound more like yourself today. I must say you sounded a little weird yesterday."

"Yes, well yesterday was yesterday. I'll call you."

Next, Manetti shredded his confessions and burned the shredded paper.

Now his big challenge was to get rid of O'Malley's body. He wondered whether he was about to pull off the perfect crime, and if not, who or what was going to trip him up. Anyway, there was no turning back. There'd be no turning back for the rest of his life. Whatever the future might bring, at least he and Pierrette were free and safe from the madman.

It was after eight when Manetti backed the Lexus down the driveway, pausing at the curb to exchange greetings with a neighbour.

Although a hearse driver should put on a solemn face, this hearse driver was smiling broadly as he headed north. O'Malley was dead, and his death was deliverance.

CHAPTER
TWENTY-EIGHT

IT WAS JUST past nine o'clock on Friday morning when Drake telephoned Macdonald. "Ross, can you come for a chat?"

In a minute or so Macdonald strode in. "What's up, Alastair?"

"I was wondering if you'd lost anything?"

"Not that I know. Why?"

Drake gestured to the receiver on his desk and watched the colour drain from Macdonald's face. "Why did you do it, Ross?"

Macdonald said nothing for a long moment and then became defiant. "I did it for the good of the company. By promoting the white-knight option, you were putting Laurentian into play—putting Laurentian at risk. I had to save the company from your reckless course of action. I did it for the good of the company."

"Very noble of you, Ross! Save Laurentian from Madman Drake. Very noble indeed! I guess that was your reason for having clandestine meetings with Noramet and Thorne Sullivan."

"How do you know about that?"

"It's my job to know what's going on—particularly what's going on behind my back."

"You were ready to gamble Laurentian's future to save your buddy Manetti, but Laurentian's not yours to gamble. Roll your own dice, not Laurentian's. Gamble with your own career, not mine."

"I never thought Laurentian was mine to gamble. My recommendation had to go to the Board, and I took it to the Board. Your recommendation should have gone to the Board too, but you stayed silent. You said nothing at the meeting, because you'd done your talking before the meeting and behind the scenes."

"So you say."

"Yes, I do say. I know because several Directors spoke to me after the meeting. They were at pains to assure me that, although they rejected the white-knight option, you hadn't influenced their decision in the slightest. You offended them. I'm afraid *you've* been gambling with *your* career, and I'm afraid you've lost the gamble." Drake handed Macdonald a single sheet of paper, which had been typed on Macdonald's letterhead.

Dear Alastair,

Having done what I set out to do at Laurentian, I think it's now time for me to move on to other career opportunities and challenges. Accordingly, I am submitting my resignation as President and Chief Operating Officer and as a Director of Laurentian Mining Inc., effective immediately.

Yours very truly,

"I typed it myself, Ross, which accounts for the rather unprofessional spacing. Sorry about that."

"What makes you think I'll sign this?"

"I rather thought you'd prefer to avoid a police investigation and the resultant scandal."

"What I did isn't illegal."

"Isn't it? I haven't consulted the Legal Department—not yet—so I'm not sure what the legal fallout will be. Shall we roll the dice and find out?"

"You've been out to get me all along, Drake, and here's your chance to do it. Before you start playing God, perhaps you'd better examine your own motives."

"I have, Ross, I have. I'll be glad to see you go, if that's what you mean. I was going to use all my considerable influence to ensure that you didn't succeed me, if that's what you mean. What's troubling me is whether or not I should play God by accepting your resignation and keeping this whole thing under wraps. Speaking as a mere mortal, my inclination is to expose you and thus forewarn the unsuspecting world of your perfidy. However, if I do that, you'll be ruined ... everywhere and forever. I decided last night to play God and give you a second chance. However, you can easily dissuade me. As far as playing God goes, you'd better pray I do."

"Who else knows about this?"

"You tell me! At Laurentian, only Jack Seagram and I know. Do you want to keep it that way, or would you prefer that I send the tape of this conversation to the Legal Department?"

"You've recorded this?"

"Of course I have, Ross. I've taken a leaf from your book."

Without replying, Macdonald picked up the pen and signed the letter.

"Date it also," instructed Drake. "Date it today."

"Don't announce this until next week," growled Macdonald. "I'll clean out my desk over the weekend."

Drake shook his head. "I'll be glad to hold off on the announcement, Ross, but you're leaving right now. You'll find Jack Seagram in your office when you return, with several transfer cases. He'll stay there while you pack your personal belongings, and he'll arrange to have them delivered to your house this morning. I've instructed him to retrieve your access keys, your company pass and your company credit cards. And I've also instructed him to stay with you until you do leave. If you don't go promptly and quietly, I've instructed Jack to have you forcibly ejected. We'll find a suitable reassignment for your secretary, so you needn't worry about her."

"I wasn't. What about my severance arrangements?"

Drake tapped the resignation letter with his pen. "What severance arrangements? I'm not firing you. You're quitting. I'll send you a rose at mid-summer, if you like."

"You really are a first-class bastard."

"On the contrary, I'm your first-class guardian angel. I could ruin you, but I'm giving you a second chance." He slid Macdonald's letter back to him. "You're free to rip it up and let the chips fly. Frankly, it would ease my conscience to let the chips fly. I have nothing to hide. Do you?"

Macdonald glared but didn't reply. He sat there for several moments, clenching and unclenching his fists. Then he stood up and stalked out.

CHAPTER
TWENTY-NINE

MANETTI WAS STILL in a buoyant mood when he reached the cottage. He and Pierrette had a leisurely lunch on the deck, during which he consoled her by elaborating on the story he'd told her on the phone: that their ageing pet had died peacefully, probably of a heart attack, and was buried in the garden.

After lunch, Pierrette drove into town for groceries, and Manetti seized the opportunity to transfer O'Malley from car to boathouse, a task much easier in contemplation than execution. The sturdy dolly was no match for the rough path that ran steeply downhill from parking lot to lake. Twice the dolly slipped sideways off the narrow path, which sent the coffin tumbling end-over-end for several runaway yards. It took a lot of manhandling to wrestle the heavy box to the boathouse, and then into the boathouse, and then into the well of the motor launch.

That done, he opened the trunk and crammed three concrete blocks on top of the corpse. He slammed and re-locked the lid, wrapped a sturdy chain four ways around the trunk, and secured it with a heavy padlock. Finally, he took up a large spike and hammered several holes in the side of the box.

O'Malley was now ready for burial at sea.

As an afterthought, Manetti picked up a discarded length of sail and draped it loosely over the trunk. It was a grungy shroud, but an effective concealment.

Sweating heavily from his exertions, he donned trunks and went for a swim. O'Malley stayed where he was, lying in state—although no one came to pay last respects.

That evening, the Manettis arrived home about eleven o'clock, having spent the evening with neighbours.

"I'm for bed. I'm dog-tired," said Pierrette.

"In that case, you're too tired for a moonlight cruise."

"Definitely! Besides, there's no moonlight. Look at those storm clouds."

"I think I'll take a spin anyway," said Manetti.

"There's weather coming. You'll get soaked!"

"After a week in the office, I crave the great outdoors."

She shrugged. "Suit yourself, but be careful! And be quiet!"

Pierrette headed for the bedroom, and he headed for the lake.

The launch lay low in the water as it slipped sluggishly out of the boathouse. Pierrette was right, a storm was brewing; the sky was black and the water was choppy. Manetti kept the launch at a slow and measured pace, a funereal pace, not out of respect for the deceased but because the boat was overloaded and the neighbouring cottagers were sleeping.

When he was well out in the lake, the storm broke. Thunder was rolling and crashing, lightning sheets were following each other in quick succession, and rain was beating down. *O'Malley's revenge,* he thought.

There'd been no turning back last night, and there'd be no turning back tonight.

In a few more minutes, he was roughly at mid-lake, a place where the charts recorded a depth of at least one hundred feet, certainly deep enough for a watery grave. He extinguished the running lights and set about his task. Jettisoning the cargo in a thunderstorm proved to be more difficult and hazardous than he'd foreseen. The pounding rain made the deck slippery, and the boat rocked and spun crazily as he wrestled with the coffin, struggling to keep his footing. After several unsuccessful attempts, he got the trunk standing on end, which brought him face to face with the real danger: how to push it into the lake without capsizing. There was no safe way to ease the trunk overboard, so he threw caution to the wind once more and shoved it with all his strength. It was a foolhardy manoeuvre that almost capsized the boat, and sent Manetti as well as the trunk flying into the lake.

He surfaced, choking and disoriented. It took a long minute before he spotted the dark shadow of the launch, now about fifty feet from him and drifting smartly away. Fighting back panic, he struck out for the boat, which continued to drift away at a fast clip. He was swimming for his life.

He swam as hard as he could and as long as he could before looking again. The gap had narrowed to about twenty feet, close enough to give him hope and second wind. He swam hard again and overtook the boat. Grabbing the stern, he hung on desperately, drifting with the boat for a long time before he could summon the strength to haul himself aboard.

Like a madman, he stood in the drifting boat, oblivious to the beating rain and lightning flashes, shouting wildly, "Rot in Hell, O'Malley! Rot in Hell, you psycho bastard!"

After several minutes, Manetti recovered his sanity. He moved to the driver's seat, started the engine, and headed for home. As he sped around the point, he saw lights at the boathouse, a welcome beacon to guide him, but also a warning beacon that Pierrette was waiting for him.

As he slowly manoeuvred the boat into its berth, she was there, arms crossed, eyes glaring. "I was about to send out a search party," she said.

"Who's missing?" Seeing that her relief was about to give way to anger and tears, he held up both hands in a gesture of truce. "Look, we're both tired, so let's fight in the morning." Without replying, she turned heel and left.

Manetti secured the launch and returned to the cottage, which was entirely dark—Pierrette's silent reproach. After a long shower, he poured himself a beer and sat in the dark living room, thinking about what had happened and wondering what was going to happen. Maybe he'd committed the perfect crime, maybe he hadn't. Maybe he'd committed two perfect crimes, maybe he hadn't. He'd just have to stay the course.

He finished his drink and went quietly to bed. In a couple of minutes, there was a voice in the darkness. "I can't sleep," she said.

"I thought you were dog-tired."

"I was, before you got lost at sea, you silly bugger. Now I can't sleep."

"I didn't know you cared."

"I was worried about the launch. It's a very expensive boat."

"Yes, well it's insured, and so am I for that matter. If we'd been lost at sea, you'd have become a wealthy widow with many suitors and lots of insurance money to buy another launch." He reached across and stroked her hair. "If you're going to toss and turn anyway, why don't we toss and turn in unison?"

They did, and afterwards, they both slept peacefully.

CHAPTER
THIRTY

IT WAS MONDAY evening. Fennell was sprawled on a chesterfield, half watching television. He was restless and dissatisfied. He liked the King Edward Hotel, and he liked the suite well enough, except that it reminded him of Noramet's apartment, which in turn reminded him of Susan. He felt listless and lonesome, a concupiscent Napoleon without his Josephine.

Just a couple of hours earlier, the Noramet jet had whisked him from New York to Toronto for his Tuesday showdown meeting with Manetti. Contrary to what he'd told Manetti, he had no other business in Toronto. Now it was eight o'clock, and he was killing the evening alone.

If only he'd brought Susan along.

In an attempt to stifle his sexual yearnings, he turned his mind to tomorrow's meeting. Now that Laurentian had bowed out, he was sure Lunex would capitulate and sell the Mountain Lake properties. Fennell would be gracious in victory, as he always was on such occasions. He enjoyed playing the magnanimous conqueror, a role he'd played many times before. Manetti and Ransom wouldn't bow their heads and kiss his ring, but so what? Surly capitulation was just as good to him as servile capitulation. Either way, it wouldn't take long. The Noramet plane would be waiting to fly him to Newark, where his driver would be waiting to drive him to Park Avenue, where

Susan would be waiting to welcome him home. There'd be sex and champagne to celebrate yet another corporate acquisition—probably his last corporate conquest, but definitely not his last sex and champagne celebration.

If only he'd brought Susan along.

The telephone interrupted his musings.

"Yes!"

"Hello, Richard Fennell, I'm a voice from the past."

"Forgive me, I don't recognize the voice."

"Moira Fitzgerald."

"Moira! Is it really you?" Fennell stood up. "And if it is really you, where are you?"

"Downstairs in the lobby."

"Well then, come right up! I'm in 814. This is wonderful!"

"I think you'd better come down. I'll be in the Consort Bar."

"Come up! I insist!"

"I'll be in the Consort Bar," she replied.

"Have it your way. I'll be right down."

Fennell hung up with a smirk. He hadn't anticipated an eleventh-hour manoeuvre from Lunex, but here it was. They were evidently sending Moira to sue for mercy. He wondered what she'd say, and whether she was still beautiful. He'd string things along and see where they led. Perhaps they'd lead back to the suite for a nightcap, and perhaps they'd lead from the living room to the bedroom. A dull evening was suddenly coming alive.

Leaving Susan in New York had been a good idea. He congratulated himself.

In a few minutes, Fennell brushed past the *maître d'* and strode into the bar. Completely ignoring the aficionado and his ingratiating welcome, he made a beeline for Moira's table. "Moira, I can't tell you how happy I am to see you again." He stooped and kissed her on the cheek and then sat down. "I've gone grey since you left me. You're as beautiful as ever."

"'In the dusk with the light behind me,' as Mr. Gilbert would say."

"There's lots of light in here, Moira Fitzgerald. Lots of light. I can't believe it. My Moira! The same Moira!"

"Not the same Moira. I'm a middle-aged matron with two teen-aged sons."

"I wish they were mine."

"Do you remember Warren Ransom?"

"Yes, indeed, although he wasn't with us long. And now he's president of Lunex."

She nodded. "You know we're married, right?"

"I was recently apprised of that sad fact."

"Why *sad?* I'm happy."

"And so is Warren Ransom, I venture. It is I who's sad. I've never understood why you left me."

"I think you do."

"You knew how I felt."

"I knew what you wrote."

"I meant every word of that letter. Every single word. Why didn't you reply? Why didn't you return my calls?"

"I had nothing to say."

"I thought we loved each other. We made love that afternoon."

"We had sex that afternoon. That's why I'm here. So, as you used to like to say, *let's get right down to business.*" She handed him a letter and watched him closely as he read it. "That's a photocopy, if you'd like to keep it for your records."

"It's not at all what you think, Moira. Believe me. It's not at all what you think."

"What do you mean *what I think?* It's not a matter of opinion. It's a matter of scientific fact. It says I was intoxicated with a drug I'd never even heard of, much less ingested voluntarily. A fourteen-letter drug, which only a pharmacist can pronounce and only a rapist would use."

"This is awful!" Fennell covered his face with his hands for a moment. "It's not what you think."

"I *think* facts are facts. You're holding a medical report. You're *holding* a fact."

He laid the letter face down on the table. "If you'd told me before, I could have explained."

"The doctor did all the explaining."

"I didn't use the drug to seduce you."

"You used it to flavour the champagne."

"Our lovemaking was entirely consensual, and you know it."

"I was drugged. Read the report!"

"Be fair! You weren't a child. You responded. You were fully conscious."

"*Fully* conscious or *drugged* conscious? *Free* consent or *drugged* consent? *Consensual* sex or *rape*? I was just another notch on your gun. Yes, I responded, that's the terrible part. I've lived my life not knowing whether I was unfaithful to Warren or whether I was raped. That's the horror I've had to live with."

"I used the drug to make things easier. It's just a relaxant. I mean, it was our first time together, and we were in my office. It was awkward."

"*Awkward!* Then why didn't you drug *yourself?*"

"Be fair!"

"One drugs dumb animals to subdue them, but I'm not a dumb animal."

"Be fair! You weren't inexperienced."

"Except for that hateful encounter with you, my *experience* was and is limited to Warren, whom I love and cherish."

"I honestly believed you wanted to make love. I knew it would be awkward for both of us—I mean the place, the circumstances generally—which is why, and the only reason why, I added a few drops of relaxant to your champagne. I'd had several glasses before you showed up, and my judgement was obviously clouded, but at the time, I honestly believed you wanted to make love. I used the relaxant to ease your inhibitions, not to overcome resistance. I was in love with you. I still am."

"You were in lust, and then, having seduced me, you got nervous. That's why I sent your cheque to the Rape Crisis Centre."

"To punish me? To intimidate me?"

"No, because it seemed like the right place for it. I didn't want your money. Do you think I'm a whore? I just wanted to be quit of you."

"Be fair! If I'd intended to seduce you, wouldn't I have set the scene for a seduction? Wouldn't I have lured you to my office?"

"I was a windfall seduction."

There was a long pause before he responded. "Well, you've been quit of me for well over twenty-five years. So, why are you here tonight? I think I know the answer, but let's hear it from you."

"I know why I'm here, but I'm not quite sure what you'd call it." She toyed with her glass for a moment and then looked him in the eye. "I suppose you'd call it blackmail, although I certainly don't want any money from you."

"You want Noramet to abandon its takeover plans."

She nodded.

"I thought I knew all the takeover defences, but this is a new one. Anyway, as I told Manetti last Thursday, Noramet will happily abandon its takeover plans if Lunex sells us the Mountain Lake properties. I rather suspect that Manetti and your husband have decided to do just that. Have they?"

"I have no idea what they've decided, but you know what I mean, and what I want."

"Manetti and your husband must be desperate to use you like this. It's despicable."

"Nobody's *using* me. In my whole life, the only person who ever *used* me was you. Warren doesn't know I'm here. Neither does Rocco. I'm here on my own account."

"Does your husband know we made love?"

"He knows we had sex. I told him that very evening."

"For the record, I didn't know you were engaged to him, or anyone else for that matter."

"Which made me fair game."

"I didn't say that or mean that. Does he know about the drug?"

"No. I didn't know about the drug for several days ... until I got the medical report. I thought I'd been unfaithful to him, and I made no excuses. Perhaps I *was* unfaithful to him. The drug makes everything ambiguous. The nightmare is that I've never known for sure."

"Why didn't you tell him about the drug when you did find out?"

"Several reasons. Commingled reasons. By the time I received the medical report, the damage was done, and it would have sounded like a belated excuse—an after-the-fact rationalization. By then, we'd worked through the trauma, although it's always lurked in the background of our marriage. However, the most urgent reason was my fear that he might attack you. That he might kill you. I still have that fear. I'm speaking quite literally when I say that, so please believe me. However, if you and Noramet don't leave Lunex alone, if you don't go away and stay away, then I'm prepared to tell the world."

"Brave girl, but please believe *me* when I tell you that I'm not a bit afraid of your husband or *the world*. I very much doubt the world is interested. I very much doubt our coupling is newsworthy after all these years, except to your family and friends."

"I'm not newsworthy, but you certainly are. You're Richard Fennell the third, Connecticut socialite, Chairman and Chief Executive Officer of giant Noramet Inc. You're newsworthy all right. Just one anonymous letter to the gutter press will be like throwing a lighted match on gasoline. I could write the headlines myself: *Chairman of Noramet drugs and rapes secretary.* I bet they'd come up with better headlines than that one."

"Your word against mine."

"My word and the medical report against yours."

"You can't prove I administered the drug."

"My word and the medical report and Albert's against yours. Do you remember Albert?"

"*Albert?* My old driver?"

She nodded.

"Albert wasn't there."

"How do you think I ended up in the hospital? You had Albert drive me home that afternoon, and I passed out in the car. Albert got nervous and drove me there. Not only that, he came back to the hospital and took me home. I suppose that was after he delivered you to your next *rendezvous.*"

"He didn't report that to me."

"Why would he? Albert hated you, whereas Albert and I were friends. Although I didn't tell him anything about the medical report, he apparently knew what had happened without being told. After you sacked him, he wrote me about driving your *Sleeping Beauties* home from various locales. He told me, with commendable delicacy I might add, that you used to drug your girlfriends and that he hoped I hadn't been one of your victims. He obviously knew that I *had* been one of your victims. It's a moving letter."

"I'm not the least bit intimidated by the vindictive ramblings of a disloyal servant, whom I doubtless fired for good cause. Albert's no threat. He's a disaffected ex-employee. That's all Albert is. Someone to buy off or scare off or both. I know how to deal with the *Alberts* of this world. They're a dime a dozen."

"I'm afraid you can't coerce Albert. He's dead."

"Not much use to you dead. Dead witnesses are pretty mum as a rule."

"His letter speaks volumes."

"I doubt it would be admissible in evidence."

"You're talking about court evidence. I'm talking about the media. Why would I sue you? I didn't want your money then, although I could have used it back then. I don't want your money now, and I don't need your money now. However, I'm ready, willing, and able to ruin your reputation."

"And I'm ready, willing, and able to sue you for defamation, and anyone else who publishes your libels. Not only that, but I'd press criminal charges against you. I'm calling your bluff, Moira. Believe me I am."

"And I'm calling yours. I have the documents assembled and ready to mail: an anonymous *exposé* of Richard Fennell the third. The letter's addressed to a particularly vicious New York rag, vicious even by the gutter standards of the gutter press. When they telephone me to confirm the story, I'll gasp in dismay and beg them not to publish my dread secret, which will guarantee that they'll do just that. After I tearfully confirm the truth of the story, every newspaper and internet gossip site in North America will pick it up. The story will *go viral*. I believe that's the expression. You'll be famous for all the wrong reasons. The only downsides for me are my family and friends, as you point out. However, I'll prepare them for the shock, and I'm willing to pay the price. So, go right ahead and call my bluff."

"It's hard to believe that my lovely Moira has become such a first-class bitch."

She winced, as if he'd struck her. After a long pause, she responded, as if speaking to herself rather than to him. "It seems that whenever a man fights for his interests, he's *manly*; whenever a woman fights for hers, she's a *bitch*."

"If you corner me, I'll claim we were frequent sexual partners," said Fennell, "and I'll further claim you took the drug voluntarily, as a sexual stimulant, for that's all it is. Many of my partners realize heightened sexual response by using that drug."

"First, you called it a *relaxant*, now you call it a *stimulant*. Whatever it was, I ended up in the hospital."

"A convenient way to set me up for blackmail. Watch out, Moira, you're playing with fire. If you know what's good for you, you'll back off before you get burned."

"And if you know what's good for you, you'll just disappear from my life, which means leaving Lunex alone—you and Noramet both. Just vanish!"

"Even if your threats did intimidate me, which they don't, Noramet couldn't and wouldn't be deterred by an allegation of impropriety against its Chairman, particularly when that allegation would be flatly denied and aggressively challenged by the Chairman, and particularly when the allegation would be hoary with age, and particularly when the Chairman could and would mount a very credible case that he was being blackmailed to withdraw Noramet's takeover bid."

"You couldn't prove blackmail."

"Couldn't I?" He picked up the medical report, folded it neatly, and put it in his jacket pocket. "If you weren't blackmailing me, when, where, and why did you give me the medical report? You've committed a criminal offence, and I'll see you behind bars. I could, and believe me I would, give date, time, and place to that charge. Date? Today. Time? Eight thirty p.m. Place? the Consort Bar at the King Edward Hotel. Blackmailer Moira Ransom, wife of Warren Ransom, who happens to be President and COO of Lunex. I'm afraid you and the ghost of disloyal Albert will combine to ruin Moira Ransom, not me. It'll take more than the two of you to ruin me."

"In that case, I'm glad there are more."

"This is getting curiouser and curiouser, as Alice would say. Let's hear your next threat."

"Albert named names in his letter, actually about a dozen of your ex-girlfriends. There's a sorority of your victims out there, and some of us have been comparing notes. My guess is that three or four are willing to come forward too, as long as I go first. Maybe some New York ambulance chasers will even propose a class action. That'd be a novel lawsuit. I wouldn't put it past them. This story has legs, if you'll forgive the pun."

"I don't believe you. What ex-girlfriends?"

"Drugged ex-girlfriends."

"Name them."

"So, you can *buy them off, or scare them off, or both?* Don't worry! If Noramet won't be deterred by the drugging and raping of Moira Fitzgerald, perhaps a half dozen similar complaints won't bother them either. We'll have to see."

"I'm not Noramet. I'm just an officer of the Company. No matter how much muck you rake up about me, Noramet will proceed with the takeover. That'll leave you and me to duke it out after the fact, one-on-one, and in front of the world. Let me remind you that I'll have a team of mean lawyers behind me—all paid for by Noramet—so I hope you have a large legal war chest. Let me remind you further that they'll portray you as a blackmailing slut, so I hope you have a thick skin, and I hope your husband and sons have thick skins too. I'd call it a lose/lose outlook for Moira Ransom and her family."

"I haven't come here on the spur of the moment. I've thought it through."

"If this thing spins out of control, you'll be the big loser, and I don't want that to happen. You think I'm saying that to save myself, but believe me, I'm trying to save you. If you attack me, I'll have to defend myself and things will get down and dirty. If I'm forced to turn our lawyers loose on this, there'll be more than one Hound of the Baskervilles to tear you to shreds, and I won't be able to stop them."

"This is my only weapon, and I'm prepared to use it, and I'm prepared to suffer the consequences. Your lawyers may be ravenous hounds, but the truth is the truth, and the truth is that you drugged and raped me. I'll have lawyers too."

"Since Noramet will acquire the Mountain Lake properties in any event, what's the point of scorched-earth litigation? No matter who wins, everybody loses at litigation. Everybody but the lawyers. If you play ball with me, nobody loses. I'll make Warren Executive Vice President of Operations for Noramet. That's a smaller title but a much bigger job than President of Lunex, and it pays a lot more, and it would put him on track to becoming President and Chief Operating Officer. Not only that but Warren would be in charge of the Mountain Lake properties and oversee their development. Warren's a good man, and we've had our eye on him. I'd make that appointment with pleasure, in spite of your threats, not because of them."

"He'd never work for Noramet."

"An eye-popping career opportunity might change his mind. However much Warren hates me, I'll soon be retiring; everybody knows that. All that aside, no matter how much he hates Noramet and me, think of how a public scandal will affect him and your sons. Whatever accusations you may choose to hurl at me will be twisted and spun to your disadvantage. My lawyers will make Jezebel look like a choir girl in comparison to you. I shudder to think of my wife, anyone's wife, under that kind of legal assault. They're not lawyers; they're hunting hounds. Think of how Warren will suffer."

"I have. I am."

"And you don't care?"

"I care deeply. I'm gambling that Noramet will back off."

"You'll lose your gamble, and win disgrace."

"We'll see. Based on your glistening brow, I think I must be on the right track."

"You really hate me, don't you?"

"Hate is a shifty word, like 'mugging' for 'robbery,' like 'lovemaking' for 'rape.' If 'hate' presumes emotional involvement, then I certainly don't hate you, any more than I ever loved you. At the risk of bruising your ego, I don't think of you at all, not as a person. Although I've never been able to forget or forgive what you did to me, or what I let you do to me."

"You've demonized someone who loved you deeply, and who still loves you deeply. How can I make you believe that?"

"By abandoning your takeover plans. By going away and staying away." She stood up abruptly. "I've said what I came to say, and I've heard what you've had to say. Anything more is just argument, and I haven't come here to argue."

"Yes, I guess there's nothing more to say." He summoned the waiter and signed the check. "I'll walk you to your car."

"No need! I'm parked just along the street."

"I need to stretch my legs and get a breath of fresh air—fresh smog I should say. We're having a heat wave in New York too."

They walked in silence until she stopped beside a BMW convertible.

"Nice car," he said. "With two teenaged sons, I might have expected an SUV full of sports equipment, and a Labrador retriever."

"We have an SUV and a collie. By the way, she's a bitch too, and has been known to bite when threatened."

"I'm not afraid of your bite, Moira. I'm afraid of having to put you down. If I ask you a question, will you give me an honest answer?"

"I've been honest with you so far."

"If I did arrange for Norametto abandon the takeover, and I probably could, would you accept that as an act of love and contrition on my part, or would you think I'd caved in to your threats?"

"How could I know your motives?"

"That's a question, not an answer. Could you believe I'd done it because I love you, and for no other reason? Please give me an honest answer. It matters to me, because I love you, whether you believe it or not, and it matters to me … because I'm not a rapist, no matter how you construe what happened. I loved you when you were with me at Norametto, long before that afternoon, and I've loved you ever since. I've never stopped loving you, Moira."

She looked directly into his eyes. "Are you being honest with me now, or are you just playing a role? Or do you know the difference?"

"I'm dead honest, Moira."

"Maybe you are … maybe you're not." She pressed the release and he held the door for her. She started the car and lowered the window.

"Yes, if you and Noramet leave Lunex alone, I'll construe that as an act of love and contrition on your part."

"Thank you for that. We've both said hard things, things we shouldn't have said, so let's make peace. Why don't you come up to my suite for a nightcap?"

"I really have to be going. We live in Oakville."

"You're asking me to persuade Noramet to abandon its takeover bid at the eleventh hour—indeed at five minutes to midnight. That's a tall order. How can I persuade Noramet to do a U-turn if I can't even persuade you to have a nightcap and bury the hatchet? What are you afraid of?"

"Well, Richard Fennell, since you're looking for honest answers, I'm afraid you want to bury the shaft rather than the hatchet." She smiled demurely, the window slid shut, and the car eased into the King Street traffic.

CHAPTER
THIRTY-ONE

FENNELL WALKED SLOWLY back to the hotel and returned to the Consort Bar, again bypassing the maitre d', who glared at him but dared not do more. Their recently-vacated table had been cleared but was unoccupied, so he took it, ordered a cognac, and settled back to muse on this change of events.

Too bad Moira hadn't bought into his undying love routine, especially since it was a little bit true really. He felt a sense of undying love for all of his ex-mistresses, and he felt a sense of undying love for Moira too, even more so because she'd never been his mistress. Too bad she'd never been his mistress. Too bad she'd seen right through his clumsy seduction attempt tonight. Ah well, no one ventured, no one vanquished. Another time, different circumstances, and he'd have had her.

He had to make a big decision by tomorrow morning, and he was forced to admit that Moira had shaken him with her threats, her grim resolve, and her damned medical report. He took the report from his jacket and read it again, shaking his head in frustration as he did so. Then there was Albert. How much had Albert actually known? How much had Albert actually said?

Then there were his ex-mistresses. Was Moira bluffing about some of them being ready to settle scores with him? Perhaps she wasn't.

Would she make good on her threats? Perhaps she would. He'd seen steely determination in her eyes, and he knew from bitter experience that an enraged woman is beyond fear and reason. Even if his lawyers shot the charging tigress, his reputation would be shot dead too.

What if the sisters of vengeance were indeed out to get him? He'd parted company with a dozen and more mistresses over the years, always on generous terms and usually on friendly terms—but not always on friendly terms. He had routinely used that drug as a sexual condiment, and if other sex partners came forward with similar accusations, it would weaken his claim that Moira was just a liar and a blackmailer. He might be able to discredit one Moira but not several Moiras. And if a few of his ex-mistresses caught the scent of money, it would be expensive to buy them off, assuming he *could* buy them off. He'd be bidding for their silence against the scum media, which would be bidding for their exclusive stories.

His disgrace would disgrace his wife and daughter. Elizabeth had always known he was a philanderer, but the world at large didn't know. If more *victims* came forward, a bad situation would spin out of control and become a sleazy sex scandal. How many charging tigresses would his lawyers be able to cut down? There'd be lots of lawyers, lots of legal huffing and puffing, threats and posturing, denials and spin-doctoring, statements of claim and statements of defence, but at the end of the day, in fact quite early in the day, the court of public opinion would convict him and crucify him. Half the world would condemn him, and the other half would ridicule him.

If he didn't back down, his legacy would be forever tainted by scandal. He'd be forever remembered and laughed at as Richard (Date Rape) Fennell. On the other hand, if he did back down, he and Doyle would have a hell of a time concocting a business rationale for Noramet's change of direction. Doyle was shrewd and perceptive and would put two and two together. In fact, he'd put two and two together already. So what? Why should he care what Doyle knew or Doyle thought? Fennell was the boss. Doyle was his man.

He reminded himself that he'd never backed down from a fight before. Why now? He was a good fighter, and whenever circumstances called for dirty fighting, he excelled at dirty fighting. He had always prided himself on his killer instinct. Why would he run away with his tail between his legs? Charging tigresses be damned! Their complaints, however they chose to spin them, would be every bit as embarrassing to them as they would be to him. Moreover, their grievances would all be stale-dated, and suspect for that.

Only Moira had been a one-night stand—in her case, a one-afternoon stand. The rest had been proper affairs, which had budded, blossomed, faded, and died, as proper affairs should. None of his ex-mistresses could cry rape in the context of a two-or-three-year affair, at least not convincingly. Not one of them had been a choir girl when he took her up, and not one of them—not to mention their subsequent husbands and families—would relish their depictions as promiscuous sluts.

To succumb to the threats of a blackmailer would be cowardly, and he wasn't a coward. If Moira dared to start a fight, he'd damn well finish it. He'd expose her for the blackmailer she was and teach the bitch a lesson.

Fennell left the bar and crossed the lobby to the elevators, still lost in thought, still of two minds. He decided to let his subconscious sort things out overnight. The Almighty would surely step in and send him a signal while he slept. The Almighty had never failed him in the past. After all, the Almighty was a Republican, an Episcopalian, and a charter member of Noramet's Advisory Board.

As she drove along the Queen Elizabeth Way, Moira Ransom was also musing on the interview. She was in equal parts offended, amused, and flattered by the old lecher's declaration of undying love, and his transparent attempt to get her into bed. At the not-so-tender age of fifty, she was apparently still a temptress—albeit to a man who would hit on a plastic mannequin if it was wearing a skirt.

Although she hadn't believed for a minute that the old satyr had been carrying a torch for her all these years, she was quite happy if he believed it. Fantasy is a potent aphrodisiac. If he had really been nurturing that fantasy all these years, her parting shot had been a serious *faux pas*. The right step would have been to look soulful, tearful, and demure, but it was too late for dissembling now. The insult had been spontaneous, well-aimed, and well-deserved, albeit unladylike. She chortled to herself, but it was a nervous chortle.

Moira was forced to admit that Fennell had shaken her confidence. Her threat hadn't seemed to faze him at all. If Noramet proceeded against Lunex, Fennell was right that her retaliatory strike wouldn't save Lunex. If it was a victory at all, it would be a pyrrhic victory. What would it avail her? Nothing but grief! She would be the central and lonely figure in a sordid sex scandal.

Although she had talked to four of his ex-girlfriends, she doubted they would back her up when the chips were down. Two of them had admitted to taking the drug with full knowledge and consent; they liked the effect. The other two thought—but weren't sure—that Fennell might have drugged them, but they didn't seem too concerned one way or the other. It was history. She doubted that any of them would expose herself to the salacious media in order to support Moira Ransom. Why should they?

Her counter-strike would embarrass Fennell but that's about all. And it would do much more damage to her and her family—much more. She didn't doubt for a minute that Fennell's lawyers were attack dogs who would rip her to shreds in court. They'd demand to know why she'd withheld her complaints for the better part of three decades. Then they'd answer their own question by labelling her a blackmailer. It hadn't occurred to her that Fennell might sue her, nor had it occurred to her that she might be exposing herself to criminal charges. She needed legal advice but didn't know where to turn. She certainly couldn't divulge this mess to their family lawyer. She trusted his discretion but wouldn't be able to look him in the face again.

Then there was the matter of Fennell's job offer to her husband. She was sure Warren wouldn't accept a position with Noramet, but the offer was his to refuse, not hers.

All of a sudden, she was feeling less like the victim and more like the criminal. In this *boys will be boys* world, Fennell's treachery would be twisted and spun until it became her promiscuity.

Apart from all that, what would it cost in hard cash? She couldn't even guess how high the Ransom legal costs might soar—certainly high enough to inflict a financial body blow. She and Warren were affluent, but they didn't possess unlimited wealth. Fennell's lawyers could complicate and prolong any legal proceedings in order to weaken the Ransom resolve and resources. It would be a legal siege and a media circus, with Noramet footing the legal bill for Fennell, and the only beneficiaries would be the media and the lawyers.

Warren would stand by her with stoical fortitude, but it would be a strain on him and their marriage. How would he react to the revelation that she'd been drugged? What excuse did she have for withholding that fact from him all these years? It could only undermine his trust in her.

What would he do when he learned the truth? What if he did go gunning for Fennell? The problem with strong, steadfast, and self-contained people—people like Warren—was that there was no way to gauge their breaking point until it was too late. *"Beware the fury of a patient man."* She had rarely seen his fury, but it was something to be wary of.

Apart from all that, their sons would suffer terribly. Their schoolmates would taunt them with unspeakable slurs on their mother.

Her only hope was that Fennell was in fact living the *unrequited love* fantasy and would spare Lunex to prove his love, notwithstanding her crude insult. It was a slim hope but her only hope. She'd know tomorrow.

By the time she neared Oakville, Moira Ransom realized that her threat to expose Fennell was nothing more than a threat to expose herself, and she believed that Fennell had seen right through her. He was powerful and ruthless, someone to be feared. She feared him. By the time she wheeled into the garage, she knew that Fennell had called her bluff.

CHAPTER
THIRTY-TWO

FENNELL'S SUBCONSCIOUS FAILED to sort things out overnight. Apparently, the Almighty had been sleeping too.

At seven o'clock, he was in the shower, still trying to decide which way to jump—a study in indecision. At eight o'clock, shaved and half-dressed, he was pacing the room like a caged animal, pausing occasionally to eat something from the breakfast trolley. The decision-deadline was looming, and apparently, he'd have to make the decision without coaching from the AWOL Supreme Being. Perhaps the Almighty had been signalling him, and perhaps he'd been too preoccupied to catch the signal. He began searching for the missed signal, and he found it on the front page of the *New York Times*, which lay neatly furled beside the breakfast tray. There it was, a screaming headline: MINING DISASTER.

At some time in your callow youth, you may have briefly chinned yourself to the fantasy that you are the creature for whom Creation was created. Anyone who has ever nurtured that fantasy will understand how and why Fennell could believe that the Great Chairman and CEO of Heaven and Earth had sacrificed fifty-two miners in Pennsylvania for the sole purpose of signalling Fennell that Project Otter would be a mining disaster for him.

He stared hard at the headline, then leapt to his feet and addressed the coffee pot. "There's my signal. There's my answer. The

Lord moves in strange ways. Indeed He does." Fennell contemplated his deliverance for a few minutes before telephoning Doyle. "I've changed my mind about Project Otter. I think Noramet should reassess the geo-political risks."

"Geo-political risks?" echoed Doyle. "Mountain Lake's in Canada, Dick. I hate to admit it, but we're safer in Canada than we are in the good old U.S.A."

"Maybe yes, maybe no. In any event, I've decided to reassess Project Otter."

Doyle was shaking his head in disbelief. "When you left here yesterday, you were gung-ho."

"Yes, and now I'm not. I think Project Otter could be a mining disaster for us. Look, I don't intend to debate the issue with you. I want you to call Manetti and cancel the appointment. Tell him I've had to return to New York, and that we won't be proceeding with the Mountain Lake matter *at the present time*. That's what I want you to tell that bastard Manetti, and that's all I want you to tell him: '*We're not proceeding at the present time*.'"

"Whatever you say," replied Doyle, giving a Nazi salute to the wall opposite. "However, since you're in Toronto, and since Manetti knows you're in Toronto, wouldn't it be courteous for you to make the call?"

"Indeed, it would! That's why I'm not going to make the call."

Doyle saluted again. "Just so I understand, are we *postponing* Project Otter or scrubbing it altogether?"

"For your information, *and your information only,* I've decided to scrub it altogether."

Doyle's only response was a faint whistle of astonishment.

"I assume that was a whistle of elation," said Fennell. "You've never liked Project Otter."

"You're right about that."

"Which is the main reason I've decided to cancel it."

Doyle scrawled *bullshit* on his telephone pad. "If we're cancelling Project Otter, why not tell Lunex and put an end to it? Why not put them out of their misery? They can do a friendly merger with Laurentian and get on with life."

"I have no intention of putting Lunex out of its misery. To the contrary, I intend to extend their misery as long as possible. Bugger Lunex! Bugger Manetti! Let the bastards stew in their own juices."

"Okay, I'll tell Manetti you're en route to New York and we won't be proceeding with the Mountain Lake matter at the present time. But let's face it, Dick, sooner or later, we'll have to tell the street that we're not proceeding. Rumours are flying."

"Let them fly! We don't comment on rumours. Sooner or later, we'll tell the street, but later rather than sooner … much later. I'm not in any mood to read in the financial press that *David Slew Goliath*, so we'll stall as long as possible. In the meantime, we'll have to develop convincing reasons for reversing our ground. I admit *geopolitical risk* is a stretch. I'll leave it to your fertile mind to develop a hard-nosed business rationale, one which can withstand skeptical analysis from our Board as well as the investment community. Make it good!"

CHAPTER
THIRTY-THREE

IT WAS ABOUT ten-thirty when Doyle called Lunex.

"Top o' the mornin', Tim," said Manetti. "Our good friend Fennel hasn't shown up yet. Is that why you're calling?"

"Yes, Dick had to leave early and asked me to call you."

"By the way, Warren Ransom's with me. I'll put you on the speaker phone."

"Greetings, Tim," said Ransom.

"Morning, Warren. It's been years since I last talked to you guys."

"I'm glad Fennell's not coming," said Manetti. "We'd rather surrender to you. We've decided to tender to a Noramet bid for Lunex, assuming it's a decent cash bid and there are no better offers. You can make it a cash or share bid, but we don't want any Noramet shares."

"I'm hurt!" chuckled Doyle. "However, don't surrender too soon. We've decided not to proceed with the takeover *at the present time.* That's why I'm calling."

"What's changed since last Thursday?" asked Ransom.

"We've decided not to proceed with the takeover at the present time ... that's what's changed."

"Thanks for the clarification," said Ransom.

"I smell a rat," interjected Manetti, "and the rat is *present time.* Just how long does *present time* last?"

"Don't know."

"Don't know or won't say," retorted Manetti. "On Thursday, Fennell was a tiger, poised to pounce. Now he's apparently lost interest in the kill. Now you tell us *you're not going to proceed with the takeover.*"

"Yes, at least for the present time," responded Doyle.

"That's not good enough," said Manetti. "We're entitled to know what 'present time' means. If it just means a postponement of execution, then tell us. We'd be ecstatic if 'present time' means 'never' but we're not that lucky."

"Who knows about luck?" replied Doyle. "Look, we've *decided not to proceed at the present time.* I can't comment further."

"Do you mind if I comment further?" asked Manetti.

"Go ahead!"

"I'm going to level with you, Tim, because Warren and I both know you're a straight arrow—as straight as Fennell is crooked. If Fennell is playing cat-and-mouse with us—"

"A minute ago, he was a tiger," interrupted Doyle.

"More like the rat I smell," responded Manetti. "However, if Fennell's playing tiger-and-mouse with us, then we want to know, and we're entitled to know. The mutual antipathy which Fennell and I enjoy—and I should include Warren in the Fennell fan club—is no justification for perverting the affairs of a publicly-traded corporation."

"So, you're telling us to shit or get off the pot," said Doyle.

"Precisely," replied Manetti. "You know that Laurentian won't be our white knight. That you know."

"Right," said Doyle.

"And ... since someone's been leaking information ... you probably know that Laurentian's willing to enter into a friendly merger with Lunex, if Noramet's bid doesn't materialize."

"I've heard a rumour to that effect. Is it true?"

"You know damn well it's true, and you know we want to merge with Laurentian, so Fennell's message is vague, uncertain, and unacceptable."

"Don't kill the messenger."

"Tim, you're not a messenger boy. You're President of Norametr, and unlike Fennell, you're a principled person."

"And you want to know what the *principled President of Norametr* thinks," replied Doyle.

"Precisely! That bastard Fennell isn't going to leave us twisting in the wind like this. Either launch your bid or leave us alone. I don't know how we're going to force Noramet's hand, but I know we will."

"Look, the message was to tell *'that bastard Rocco Manetti'* that Noramet won't be *'proceeding at the present time.'* I've delivered the message."

"That's it then," replied Manetti.

"Yes, as far as *that bastard Rocco Manetti* is concerned, that's it," said Doyle. "However, the message was for you, not *that bastard Warren Ransom*, so why don't you get the hell off the line, so I can talk to Warren in private."

Manetti pressed a button and handed the receiver to Ransom.

"Okay, Tim, we're off the speaker phone," said Ransom. "What do you want to tell this bastard that you wouldn't tell the other bastard?"

"Nothing, unless we're strictly *off the record.*"

"Agreed, except that I'll be sharing it with Rocco."

"Understood. *Off the record* means I won't admit to or even remember this conversation."

"Agreed."

"Okay, let's assume I was of the view—*my personal view* you understand—that *present time* does in fact mean *never.* If you pressed me on the point, what would I do?"

"I hope you'd say so, albeit *off the record.*"

"Wrong! I'd be forced to cut you off by hanging up in disgust."

"I see," replied Ransom. "In that case, I put it to you, Tim, that *present time* does in fact mean *never,* and furthermore I press that point."

"I'm disgusted," chuckled Doyle, and then he hung up.

Ransom stared at the dead receiver and shrugged in astonishment. "It's all off the record, but it looks like we're saved, Rocco. It looks like *present time* does mean *never.*"

"Is that what he said?"

"No, but that's what he meant."

Manetti grinned, "That's good enough for me. Our luck seems to have changed."

"It's incredible!" said Ransom, still holding the dead receiver. "I wish I could tell Moira about this; I know she's been worried. However, except for you, it's all off the record."

"Surely you can at least signal her that you think everything's going to be okay. She'll read between the lines; she's a very intelligent person. As for me, it looks like I've got a career change in the offing … and so have you."

"What's that supposed to mean?" asked Ransom.

"I'll tell you later."

Printed in Canada